Killers on Elm Street Part 2

Romell Tukes

Lock Down Publications and Ca$h Presents

Killers on Elm Street 2

A Novel by *Romell Tukes*

Romell Tukes

Lock Down Publications
P.O. Box 944
Stockbridge, Ga 30281
www.lockdownpublications.com

Copyright 2021 Romell Tukes
Killers on Elm Street 2

First Edition April 2021
Printed in the United States of America

Lock Down Publications
Like our page on Facebook: Lock Down Publications @
www.facebook.com/lockdownpublications.ldp
Cover design and layout by: **Dynasty Cover Me**
Book interior design by: **Shawn Walker**
Edited by: **Jill Alicea**

Stay Connected with Us!

Text **LOCKDOWN** to 22828 to stay up-to-date with new releases, sneak peaks, contests and more...
Thank you!

Submission Guideline.

Submit the first three chapters of your completed manuscript to ldpsubmissions@gmail.com, subject line: Your book's title. The manuscript must be in a .doc file and sent as an attachment. Document should be in Times New Roman, double spaced and in size 12 font. Also, provide your synopsis and full contact information. If sending multiple submissions, they must each be in a separate email.

Have a story but no way to send it electronically? You can still submit to LDP/Ca$h Presents. Send in the first three chapters, written or typed, of your completed manuscript to:

LDP: Submissions Dept
P.O. Box 944
Stockbridge, Ga 30281

DO NOT send original manuscript. Must be a duplicate.

Provide your synopsis and a cover letter containing your full contact information.

Thanks for considering LDP and Ca$h Presents.

Acknowledgments

First and foremost, all praises are due to Allah the most high. Shout to my family for all the real love and support. Shout to my brother Smoke Black, a.k.a. Moreno from Yonkers, NY. Shout to my Yonkers niggas YB, SG, Frazier, CB, Smurff, Spayhoe, Dough Boy, Lingo, King Hound. I see you HAT, Baby James, Brisco the Makk, Bama a.k.a. Fatal Brim in the building. Shout my BK team OG Chuck- free the real; Fila, Tim Dog, Skrap from Fort Green, and my Flatbush crew. My BX niggas Melly the Makk and Jam Roc. My DC niggas La-La from Lincoln Heights, Lee Uptown, Spice Uptown, and Rellz. My Newburgh, NY niggas Spice - much love bro, facts. Thanks to all the readers – facts. I'm dropping all heat. Whenever you see my name, know it's going to be a movie. Shout to Lockdown Publications. We in the building; lock the doors gang, gang, gang... LOL. Also, big shout to Stranger from Makartor Park, Cali.

Romell Tukes

Prologue

Close to two years ago, Wolf was a college student at NYU with dreams of becoming a big-time lawyer and opening his own defense firm to help the less privileged fight criminal cases. But before he completed college, something dreadful happened. His little sister Victoria, who was on her way to a D-1 college for her basketball skills, was gunned down in front of him.

It didn't take Wolf long to find out who was responsible for his sister's death: Champ and his cousin Fred. He killed Fred first and saved Champ for later. Wolf got involved in a relationship with Bella. She was focused on becoming a cop just like her father, who was a dirty FBI agent. One day Bella's father Aguilera met with Wolf and disclosed some information that gave Wolf chills. Aguilera had seen Wolf kill Fred's and Champ's families, so he used the evidence to blackmail Wolf into killing powerful people.

While Wolf was killing drug lords, a priest, mobsters, and Mexican plugs, he found out Aguilera was a gay snake, using him to clean up his mess. Wolf met Andy and Smurf, who were both from his block on Elm Street and well-known killers and drug dealers. Andy was moving weight for Wolf while robbing big time kingpins all across New York. When he robbed and killed Ortiz, the city turned into a war zone against the MS-13 gang and Andy's crew from Elm Street. Smurf was Andy's right hand man and his business partner. Smurf was seeing so much money he didn't know how to spend it, plus it was hard to enjoy his riches when bullets were coming for his top all day.

Smurf got locked up for a parole violation for not reporting for his daily parole visits. While in Westchester County Jail, which was called Valhalla, Smurf was stabbed up by two MS-13 members, almost killing him in the gym bathroom, but luckily he survived. He ended up getting an eight month violation and he was sent to Auburn Maximum Security Prison. Smurf was in the same jail as Wolf's brother CB and the two were close.

CB was Wolf's brother. Wolf's other brother Black was a gang member and professional bank robber living in the Bronx.

Aguilera received money from an unknown source to kill Black, so he sent Wolf, unaware they were brothers. Wolf didn't kill his brother, but Aguilera made Wolf kill the mayor of Yonkers, Aguilera's longtime friend.

While Wolf was hunting down his victims, someone was trying to kill him. Aguilera gave Wolf the info of the man who was hunting him down, who was named Mickey. Wolf paid him a visit and Mickey told him the chick who wanted him dead wouldn't stop at anything to have him buried. After killing Mickey, Wolf ran into two cops. He shot one of the cops, killing him, but when he made eye contact with the other cop, his heart stopped.

The other cop was his girlfriend Bella. She had just witnessed the man she thought was a good kid kill a cop. She couldn't shoot him, so she let Wolf run.

That same night, Wolf went to Champ's aunt house and killed her while waiting on Champ. Andy had already killed Champ's mom and grandmom, so Wolf knew Champ was coming back, and he did.

Champ walked into Wolf's trap, but then Champ told him Aguilera had paid him to kill his sister Victoria just so Wolf would fall into his blackmail trap. Wolf had been played like a puppet. He killed Champ and charged it to the game.

Outside, Wolf had no clue fifty Mexicans were surrounding the area, ready to kill him but Jiménez, the Black Hand, the boss, received a call from the top dawg telling him to stand down because Wolf's father was a close friend.

Chapter 1

Attica, NY
Attica Maximum Security Prison

Lingo Loc stepped his Timbs onto the light snow on the ground at the end of May, taking a deep breath of freedom. He looked back at the huge cement wall, praying he would never have to come back because he had just had the hardest years of his life. Lingo, a.k.a. Lingo Loc, had done ten years in New York's worst state prisons, banging his Crip 8 Trey set in prisons full of Bloods who hated Crips and preyed on them. Sadly, he was stabbed on four different occasions, but he always put up a fight and still repped his Crip set. He even knocked out three so-called big homies in Sing-Sing and Wendy Prison.

He had gotten arrested at seventeen years old for shooting and drug charges. He was a loose cannon with a couple of bodies under his belt. He spend most of his time reading hood novels from Lockdown Publications and Ca$h Presents, studying, exercising, and planning for his release one day.

Lingo's girlfriend Ariana had held him down his whole bid from day one to the last day. His brother Champ played the biggest part because he was sending his brother drugs inside food packages and sending chicks up north to give him dope, weed, molly, and coke so he could live like a king.

When Lingo received the news of his mom's and grandmom's deaths, he crushed. Right after that, he heard the news of Champ's death, which was still fresh in Lingo's heart. The same week Champ was found murdered, Lingo received a letter from him informing him his days were getting short and that a nigga named Andy was the cause of everything. After Champ's death, Lingo did his research on Andy and found out a lot about him. He planned to retaliate for his family's deaths. That was the only thing on his mind.

Lingo stood at the bus stop with another inmate who had been released and was dressed in khakis and a white button up shirt.

Lingo wore a Dolce and Gabbana outfit that his boy Mack had sent him. Mack had been his childhood friend since the sandbox and Mack's sister was his girlfriend.

Lingo was medium height, brown-skinned with long dreads and tattoos covering his body. He was stocky from lifting weights when he wasn't in the box for popping shit off.

A white BMW X6 truck with tints pulled up blasting The L.O.X.'s new album. Lingo knew who it was. Yonkers niggas always played Jadakiss, Sheek, Styles PD-Block, and DMX music because they were all from Yonkers.

"Yooo, what up haaaa," Mack said in his deep voice, using his Yonkers slang.

"What's cracking haaaa," Lingo said, getting onto the black leather seats, smelling food. "What's that smell?" Lingo asked, sniffing.

"Popeye's chicken, nigga. This was a six hour ride. I tried to save you some, but you know how that be. I'm glad you made it out, bro. I heard you was in there wilding, son. Niggas said you cut Big G," Mack said, driving far away from the jail.

"Yeah, Big G was on his Blood shit, but we from Yonkers, bro. We don't see none of that gang shit when we outnumbered. We as one, son. I told him I was Cripping and he tried to line me up, so I put a scar on his face," Lingo stated.

"Damn, haaaa, Big G from the block got like forty years, right?"

"Facts. But fuck that nigga. Did you get that info?"

"Yeah. It's under your seat. You sure you want to do this on your first day out?" Mack asked. Lingo gave him an evil look. "Okay," Mack said, pulling onto the highway and turning up the music.

Mack was short, fat, ugly nigga with a gang of bitches because he had a bag. He was a big-time scammer. He had a crew of Africans in Brooklyn and the Bronx he dealt with and he was seeing big money in blue collar crime.

***

Elm Street, Yonkers

"We're here," Mack said, parking in the darkest area of the street, turning off the SUV.

"A'ight," Lingo said, grabbing the Glock 17 from under the seat and hopping out, tucking the pistol in his waistline.

Lingo walked down the empty block until he saw the house number 321. He walked up the flight of stairs and knocked on the door three times. Within seconds, an old woman with gray hair opened the door. She was wearing a gown and glasses and had a book in her hand.

"How may I help you?" she asked in a polite tone.

"Is Andy here? I'm a good friend. I've been out of state for a couple of years and I just want to check on my best friend," Lingo said.

"Oh, baby, I'm sorry. Andy hasn't lived here in years. I don't think he even lives in Yonkers no more," she said, taking off her reading glasses.

"Mom, who is that?" a deep voice said from the back room.

"It's Andy's friend – what's your name, baby?" She turned back to Lingo.

"James Bond," he said. She gave him an odd look as if he was joking, but his face was serious.

"Andy don't live here. I'm his dad, Big Bruce," the big giant said, looking Lingo up and down, knowing he was a street punk just like his son. Big Bruce had spent twenty years in the Marine Corp and now he was a vet.

"Okay," Lingo said, turning to leave. "Oh, one more thing," Lingo said, stopping, pulling out his gun.

Boc1 Boc! Boc! Boc! Boc! Boc! Boc!

Lingo made sure they were both dead by emptying the rest of the clip into both of their defunct bodies.

***

New Rochelle, NY

Next Day

Andy had had just gotten off the phone with his stepmom, who told him his father and grandmom had been murdered in cold-blooded fashion. Andy sat in his polished living room trying to hold his tears in because that was the only family he had left. Even though he and his father didn't see eye to eye, he still loved him. His grandmom was his life. She basically raised him since he lost his mother. He couldn't pinpoint who did this because he made so many enemies over the years, but he knew within time he would meet the killers.

Andy moved out of Yonkers after killing Alvarado, the Mexican boss, and Champ's mom and grandmom. He knew Yonkers wasn't safe for him or Erica. He still had his troops all over Yonkers and he was seeing big money now because he had a new plug, Trigger. Trigger was his man Lil Tom's brother, who was killed in the war with the Mexicans. Andy had traps all over Yonkers, Peekskill, Newburgh, and Mount Vernon now. Andy went to his small living room bar and poured himself a glass of the white Henny he had gotten from DR last month on his trip with Erica. All he could think about was his pops and grandmom. The pain still hadn't kicked in yet, so he was going to get drunk to wash away the pain.

Chapter 2

Yonkers, NY

"If I could go back in time, I would have been the one to take them bullets. If we knew the unseen, I wouldn't be here right now. I never had no disadvantages in life until I encounter this. Why did he take you so soon, sis? I remember one day when we was young, you said, 'Brother, life without you ain't worth living.' I feel like that every day. Sometimes I feel like killing myself, but I know that's not how the strong deal with hardship," Wolf said to his sister Victoria's gravestone, wiping his tears. Wolf came up to his sister's gravesite once a week, sometimes twice a week, when he needed someone to talk to. He always changed the flowers on her large tombstone.

"I have to go, sis. I love you. Wish me luck," Wolf said, walking off into the heat in a Tom Ford suit.

Today was a very big day for Wolf. He had been plotting this day for months, ever since Champ told him Aguilera was the one who paid to have his sister killed so he could use him. He still recently did little jobs for Aguilera here and there, but nothing too serious. Wolf played the game very well. He kept his enemies so close he was stuck to them. He building a trustworthy relationship with Aguilera and did whatever he asked, making him feel powerful and like a mastermind.

The black-on-black BMW i8 roared through the Yonkers slums, catching a lot of attention on his way to his condo on the waterfront.

His love life with Bella was good even after she saw him murder her partner in cold blood. The two never mentioned what happened that night, though she tried her best to cover up the truth. Luckily the cop killing was deemed an unsolved murder because the autopsy conducted at the crime scene by a pathologist found no type of strong evidence or DNA at the scene.

When Bella told him she was pregnant, he felt hopeless because he had unfinished business with her father. He acted as if he was excited, but deep down, he wasn't ready to bring a child into the world.

That morning, Andy had called Wolf to tell him the news about his grandmom and father. The two had built a strong bond and a trustworthy friendship. Business was amazing. Wolf was still supplying Andy with drugs he received from his missions, even with Andy having a new plug.

***

Peekskill, NY

Aguilera had just done a double at work and he felt drained as he drove back home.

Everything was perfect in his life. He had recently landed a big promotion to the chief of federal agents, thanks to some dirty work he had Wolf do for someone in the higher rankings. Wolf was like the killing machine he never had before and he planned to use him up until he felt like he didn't need him. The only thing he feared was Wolf finding out he set this whole shit up, but he wasn't alone. Recently Aguilera found out some powerful people wanted Wolf's head and there was nothing Aguilera could do about it. He dreaded having to tell Wolf because it distracted him from what Aguilera had planned for him next.

For the past couple of months, he had been fucking an FBI agent named Emmy, a beautiful blonde with a nice beach body. She was younger, and she was a trophy. The two moved in with each other and he loved having her around, not only for the wild, crazy sex, but because she was a real woman.

Aguilera pulled into his driveway, parking his Ford Explorer truck next to Emmy's Land Rover Range Rover SUV. He had bought it for her last week for her twenty-eighth birthday. He walked through his front door, turning on the porch light and living room light, wondering why Emmy had it off, but figuring she was most likely asleep upstairs. Aguilera walked into the living room and stepped in a pool of dark blood, almost tripping over Emmy's dead body, which was full of bullet holes.

"Have a seat, Aguilera. Don't worry about her, boss man," Wolf said, sitting next to the fireplace with a 50 cal with a long silencer attached to the end.

"You muthafucker!"

"Sit. I won't ask again," Wolf said, dressed in a clean suit, looking like a professional hitman.

"You think you will get away with this?"

"Aguilera, Aguilera…you don't get it, do you? It's over," Wolf said, looking at Aguilera's confused facial expression.

"I don't understand. You work for me. I call the shots!" Aguilera shouted, hitting his chest as if he was a gorilla.

"I call the shots now, you fucking gay bitch. You had me kill all those people just to hide your dirty little secrets. I can only imagine how you felt after being raped by your priest," Wolf said.

"I wasn't raped," Aguilera stated. "I fell in love. I was confused as a kid growing up. I had a rough childhood," Aguilera confessed.

"You can save your story for the RuPaul show. I just want answers. Why me, outta millions of people? Why kill my sister to get to me?"

"I see you found out. Can I at least have a drink?" Aguilera asked, looking at the rum bottle and glass on the table. Wolf poured him a glass and passed it to him, watching him gulp it down. "You were chosen since you were a kid. Your aunty trained you well in the DR every summer to be a killer."

"How do you know this?" Wolf asked. Nobody knew he used to go to train in DR with his aunty.

"Your aunty has been on the FBI's and CIA's top five list for years, but she is too brilliant to be brought down, not to mention she has lots of important people on her payroll."

"Damn." Wolf didn't know too much about his aunty except what she had told him when he was a kid.

"You have no idea who you are connected to. You may not remember, but your father Ryan is a very powerful, dangerous man. He's just like you - a hitman - but he works for powerful men."

"Thanks for the update. I'm sure I can piece together the rest," Wolf said, checking his GMT-Master Rolex watch.

"Before you kill me, you should know you have people out to kill you."

"That's my life story."

"No, Wolf, these aren't those type of people. These people will kill everything you love, including my daughter," Aguilera stated.

"Okay, but every man has his day," Wolf said, spraying seven hot bullets into Aguilera's heart, watching his body jerk for ten seconds before he closed his eyes to die.

Wolf took the stacks of folders off the table. He had found them earlier when he was searching the house for evidence that could lead Aguilera's murder back to him, but instead he found a ton of other shit that could be useful. Wolf took the rum bottle and glass because it had his DNA on it. That's why Aguilera asked him to pour him a drink: so he could leave his DNA there to get caught for his murder.

Chapter 3

Alexandra Precinct, Yonkers

Bella sat at her desk, going over the stacks of photos she had taken days ago on her stakeout. Bella had recently made detective because of the hard work she had been putting in, but being a detective was much harder than being a regular cop.

She was four months pregnant, but she was not showing yet. In a couple of days, she planned to let her boss know she was pregnant so she could take some time off. Wolf was helping her a lot with her checkups and doctor appointments and around the house. She was so happy to be carrying his baby.

Bella looked at the photos again, trying to add up everything she learned so far in the case. The photos were of Andy and the Elm Street goons selling drugs, killing, shootouts, and assaulting people. When she took this case, she thought it would be easy, but it wasn't because Andy wasn't seen selling drugs or committing any acts of violence, only his crew of over seventy niggas on one block. The photo that was taking her breath away was the photo of Andy standing in a Home Depo parking lot talking to someone. Bella knew the familiar face too well. It was Wolf, wearing a hoodie she had bought him. Bella didn't know what Wolf was into, but whatever it was, he was out of his league. She had done her best covering his tracks when he shot and killed her partner, but now he was dealing with a known kingpin her boss had an itch for.

Her cell phone rang in her purse. She thought it was Wolf, so she rushed to get it. "What? Oh my God, I'm on my way!" she yelled into the phone. It had been a call from the Peekskill police department informing her of her father's death.

Bella grabbed her purse and key, rushing out of the building, passing other officers asking her if she was okay.

***

Harlem, NY

Marvelous was in his apartment with his girl and little brother, watching the NBA playoffs, smoking and drinking.

"Son crossed King James over. I know you saw that shit, Five," Marvelous said to his little brother, pissed off that his favorite player, King James, was losing to Dewade in the Miami Heat.

"Nigga, this only the first quarter," Five replied, rolling a blunt of weed and about to hit a line of coke.

"How long is this stupid-ass game?" Destine asked. She was on her iPhone, scrolling through her social media page to see if she had any new likes on the picture of the new Birkin bag Marvelous had just bought her.

"Bitch, nobody told your ass to be out here," Marvelous said, giving her the evil eye.

"Nigga, it's my crib," Destine said. She was sitting on the couch with her knees to her chest in a pair of tiny shorts, showing her thick thighs. She was a red bone - short, thick, sexy - and a hood rat.

Before Marvelous could reply, the doorbell rang. He was waiting on his homie Fur Boy to pull up with some more bottles.

Marvelous was a plug. He sold bricks of heroin and PCP by the boat load. He had two projects that he ran: Lincoln and St. Nickolas.

Destine went to open the door without looking through the peephole, but when she saw the two police officers, she wished she had never opened the door. She had a bench warrant for boosting out of a Fendi store last summer when she was broke and down bad.

"Excuse me, but we had a call about loud noise."

"Huh?" she said nervously.

"Let me help you," one of the officers said, seeing she was lost.

Boom!

The bullet ripped through her skull and the two officers rushed into the apartment.

Boc! Boc! Boc! Boc!

Five shot at the cops, missing his target.

Boom! Boom! Boom!

Five's body fell to floor. Marvelous put his hands in the air, surrendering because he wasn't killing no cop. He preferred to get arrested and fight his charges in court.

"Where is your warrant?" Marvelous asked, not seeing any documents. Normally police had a raid warrant unless they were dirty cops.

"Where are the drugs and money?" one of the cops asked with his gun pointed at Marvelous.

"What? I don't know what the fuck you talking about, son. If you going to arrest me, do you. I got the best lawyer."

Boom!

"Ahhhhhhhhhh!" Marvelous yelled after one of the cops shot him in the foot.

"The next shot's in your head, nigga."

"Okay, okay. Everything is in the bedroom ceiling in two black garbage bags. Just don't shoot me. I got kids, bro," Marvelous cried, looking at his bleeding foot, knowing he had been set up. It couldn't have been Destine because she was dead at the front door. "I fucking hate pigs," Marvelous mumbled under his breath.

"Me too," one of the cops said while holding him at gunpoint, waiting for his partner to come back out with the mother load.

"Who sent you?" Marvelous asked.

"DeWhite."

"DeWhite? Who is that?" Marvelous asked, confused.

"DeWhite around your lips," the cop said, laughing.

"We good. Let's go, boy," the other cop said, coming out of the back room with two garbage bags full of money and drugs.

"Hold on. Y'all nigga ain't cops?" Marvelous shouted before the cops fired five rounds apiece into Marvelous's body.

***

Outside, the two cops climbed into a black Tahoe truck, driving off with someone already seated in the back seat.

"Good job. I told the both of you this was a big move," Black said from the back seat.

"Facts. You hit it right on the button," Flow said from the driver's seat, hopping on the highway to head home to the Bronx. Flow was a cocky jack boy and a hustler from the Bronx. He was tall, slim, dark-skinned with waves, and he had a scar on his face from his state bid. Flow did five years up top for robberies and while he was up top he was fucked up, so he would steal from other inmates until one caught him and cut his face out with a blade.

"I know what I know, son. Now we look forward to taking over Yonkers because this is enough keys to last us until we find a plug," Black said.

"Let's get it," Trap said in the passenger seat, taking off the fake police uniform he had bought at Party City.

Trap was Flow's brother. Both men were in their early twenties. Trap was short, brown-skinned, with hazel eyes and neat dreads. He was very handsome and had a diamond-encrusted grill in his mouth. He was a jack boy and scammer. He had no limits to get a bag and he was a cold-hearted killer.

Black had met the two of them at a bar. They tried to line him up to rob him, but Black turned the tables and robbed them instead outside of the bar. Black liked how they moved, so he gave them their shit back and took the young boys under his wing.

Chapter 4

Yonkers, NY

Rita had had just gotten off of work at 4:15 p.m. after dropping off middle school kids all around Yonkers. Now she was on her way home to take a nap. This was Rita's everyday life and she loved it because it kept her busy. Since she lived alone, she had a lot of time to spare. Every now and then she would have company, one-night stands, but nothing serious. Nobody would ever imagine she had four kids because she looked young and had a body that most women would kill for.

Since Victoria had been killed and Wolf had moved out, she was lonely. Wolf came by once a week to check on her and cook dinner. She recently heard the news about Bella being pregnant and she was happy that she was going to be a grandmom soon. She liked Bella because not only did she have a good career, but she could tell Bella really cared for her son.

Rita saw red and blue lights behind her so she pulled over so the black Crown Vic could get past her and go to wherever the officer was in a rush to. When she realized the lights were for her, she parked the car, wondering if she ran a stop sign or a red light.

The officer hopped out in plain clothes with an evil look, walking up to Rita's window. "License and registration," Sanderson said, chewing on tobacco like a true redneck.

"Sure, but why am I being pulled over?" Rita asked, looking in her sun visor for her information.

"Shut up before I pull you out and stomp the teeth out your mouth," Sanderson said.

Rita didn't say a word. Yonkers police were known for assaulting women, kids, and anybody with black complexions. She handed him everything he asked for while looking forward.

"You cleared. But tell your son Wolf I know he killed my partner after we whipped his ass that day. You might want to get your mirror fixed," Sanderson said.

"Excuse me?" Rita said before Sanderson kicked her driver's side mirror off with one powerful kick. She pulled off, wondering what Wolf had gotten himself into.

***

Sanderson had been spending months trying to figure out who killed his partner. He thought it was Sheek, whom he had killed, but Sheek was on house arrest the time Steel was murdered. One day he was lying in bed and he thought about the kid they beat up days before Steel's death. Sanderson looked into the case, researching everything about Wolf. Now Wolf was number one on his hit list.

***

Auburn Maximum-Security Prison, NY

CB was walking through the hallways on his way to the visit room. He had no clue who had come up, but he was glad because he was bored on the tier with OG Chuck talking about his war stories.

CB was getting short. He had less than three years left to go home, so he was planning on his release. Jail was jail. CB was focused on getting a bag. He had the jail flooded with heroin and weed. He and Smurf were on the same block, but Smurf was below him on the flats, which was the bottom tier where mice and roaches lived inside inmates' food and bins. Many inmates kept mice as pets.

Walking into the visit room, CB saw the last person he would ever expect to see sitting there looking at him sizing him up. "Well, well, well, look what the cat dragged in," CB said, sitting down at the table, looking at his brother Black.

"It's been a while, bro, my bad. You know how shit be in the free world," Black said.

"No, I don't, but I do know what the words family and loyalty mean and it's clear you don't. So let's get to the point. What the fuck you want?" CB said with a serious look.

"I just came to check on you, bro, that's it."

"A'ight. What's popping with Wolf and Mommy?"

"Wolf good. Last time I checked, he was cuffed and working as a pizza man. This nigga came all the way to the Bronx to deliver pizza to my crib a couple of months ago."

"Pizza? Shit, I'm hearing Wolf the man out there," CB said.

"No way, must be a different Wolf, bro. There's four Wolfs in Yonkers. Must be one of them," Black said, knowing Wolf wasn't the hustling type.

"His man Smurf in here, but he go home this week. You still robbing banks, nigga?" CB asked.

"Nah, fam, I got a new lane. I'm moving keys now," Black said, smiling.

"Damn, boy, okay. My man Two Gunz out there doing it big in the Bronx. Holla at son. He the man out there, bro. He good people. I'ma link you up with him," CB stated.

"A'ight," Black said.

The visit was cool. When it ended, they touched bases on a lot of things, then went their separate ways.

***

Days later
Auburn Prison

"Yoooo, CB, I'm out, you heard?" Smurf yelled upstairs, walking down the tier.

"A'ight, boy, hold your head up and take care of my little bro. I'll see you out there!" CB yelled.

"Facts," Smurf said, dapping up a couple of inmates he was fucking with during his time there.

Smurf was so happy he was now off parole papers so he could do as he pleased. Being in the same spot as CB was litty because he was the big homie in the prison, so whatever Smurf wanted or needed, he got it on the arm. Not only were CB and Smurf both from the same block, but Wolf was their connection. Smurf was telling CB how Wolf was giving it up on that gun game, but CB didn't believe it because Wolf was a nerd in his eyes.

Shantell, his wifey, was at work in the clothing store he gave her money to open so he planned to take the bus home to 42nd Street and meet his cousin Biggz there from Brooklyn.

Smurf changed out of his green uniform into street clothes and got his property, then rushed to the bus stop so he wouldn't miss it.

***

6 ½ hours later
42nd Street, Grand Central

Smurf walked out of the jam-packed train station to see Biggz standing across the street leaning on a new Porsche Cayenne Turbo truck with rims and tints.

"You got your weight up, son," Biggz said, embracing his little cousin. Biggz was in his early 30's and was from Flatbush in Brooklyn. He was selling pounds of weed and a little coke here and there, but nothing major. Biggz was tall, husky, with a big beard. He had a chick in Yonkers and she was telling him how niggas named Andy and Smurf were getting big money in Yonkers. He never told her how Smurf was his first cousin, so he reached out to Smurf in Downstate before he went to Auburn and kept in touch.

"You look the same," Smurf said while Biggz pulled off into traffic.

"My hoes love it. But what's up? You trying to go out? There is a party at Club Lust tonight. My man Pressure throwing a video in there too," Biggz said.

"Nah, I gotta go holler at my man Andy," Smurf said. Last week he had received a letter from Andy saying they had a problem out and he left it at that, not going into detail because Andy knew how the police in the prisons read inmates' mail.

"A'ight, got you."

"You stay in Brooklyn now?"

"Nah, I'm living with this bitch on Jackson in your hood," Biggz said.

"Oh good, now we can get this paper."

"You read my mind, nigga," Biggz said, turning up the Fabolous and Jadakiss albums.

Romell Tukes

Chapter 5

Yonkers, NY

Wolf had just left his mom's crib. She spent an hour cursing him out, telling him about her encounter with Officer Sanderson. He was shocked and denied everything. When Rita asked if he had killed a cop, he told her hell no and she believed him because he was a good kid. She asked him about his BMW i8 and he told her it was leased, which was a lie.

He was on his way home to check on Bella because since she found out about her father's death, she had been depressed and acting weird. She would leave the house at odd times of the night and come back acting unusual. With her being pregnant, Wolf knew it was a bad time for her to stress or worry. The homicide detective investigating Aguilera's murder told Bella the case would be very hard to crack because it was done by a professional and Aguilera had many enemies.

Wolf pulled into his lawyer's private garage area. Every time he looked at Bella's face, he felt a pang of guilt, but he knew there had been no other choice. All the evidence he took from Aguilera was mainly about a bunch of Mexicans from Cali and two in New York, but he also saw a pic of himself, wanted for dead by an unknown source. Whoever wanted him dead was at the top of the food chain and he wanted to know who it was.

Wolf made it inside his crib to see it was empty. Normally Bella would be on the living room couch watching Lifetime or LMN and eating something.

"Baby, where you at?" he yelled, walking around room to room.

He saw the bathroom door cracked open. He pushed it open slowly to see Bella slumped near the toilet with a needle in her left arm and in a semi-comatose state. "Bella, babyyy!" he yelled, feeling the main artery on her neck to see if she had a pulse. Luckily, she did. He called 911 and took the needle, belt, and heroin from her so the police wouldn't arrest her.

Five minutes later, Bella's chest was being pumped as she stopped breathing and flat-lined. They rushed her to the local hospital up the street, hoping to save her life.

***

Elm Street, Yonkers

"This block is crazy. I never saw so many fiends in my life, bro," Mack told Lingo, who was watching the block do numbers all day.

Lingo had to admit Elm Street was a gold mine. Niggas were trapping hard out of every building in the one block ratio. Lingo only had one thing on his mind and that was Andy and his crew. He had many sleepless nights in his cell thinking about giving him a slow death.

"You heard me?" Mack said, snapping Lingo out of his daze.

"Nah, son, what you say?"

"There is a big party in the Bronx and Yonkers next weekend. I heard both of them shits going to be turned up, You tryna slide?" Mack asked.

"I don't party, homie. I'm on a mission."

"Nah, nigga, my sister got your ass on lock. I'm surprised she not blowing your phone up now."

"Facts, bro. I can't even leave the crib without filling out paper and calling in," Lingo said, speaking the truth because Ariana was a crazy bitch.

"How you want to do this shit tonight?" Mack asked, ready to put in some work.

"Just hold me down, son," Lingo said, looking through the dark streets flooded with fiends looking like zombies.

"Let's do this fast. You got the silencers?"

"Yeah," Mack said, passing him a silencer to put on his FN weapon that held 223 bullets.

They hopped out and made their way into one of the busy buildings, where traffic was heavy at all day.

Lingo and Mack walked inside to apartment hallway to see four young'uns counting money and sharing a bottle of Henny.

"What's good, haaaa, what y'all need, fam?" one of the young niggas asked, pulling out a Ziploc bag full of weed and another bag full of bundles of heroin.

"Nah, son, they look like smokers," Zay said, pulling out a Ziploc bag full of crack in sandwich baggies - everything from dimes to forty pieces.

"I just need one of you to send a message to Andy," Lingo said.

They looked at each other, putting their drugs up just in case he tried something funny.

"We don't know no Andy, but this is my building. What's up? You got a problem or something?" Zay, the oldest of the crew, said, pulling out a pocketknife because the guns were all outside just in case the police raided the spot.

Lingo and Mack both pulled out their weapons, riddling Zay with bullets, making the small hallway look like an early 4th of July. One of the niggas tried to run until Lingo fired five rounds into his back, then he shot another one in his head, taking his head clean off his shoulders.

"I guess you will be the lucky one to tell Andy that Lingo Loc looking for him in regards to Champ," Lingo said coldly, pointing his gun at the fat scared kid, whose eyes were about to pop out of their sockets.

The kid nodded his head, unaware he was pissing on himself.

"You might want take care of that first," Mack said, pointing at the waterfall running down the kid's skinny jeans before leaving.

Romell Tukes

Chapter 6

St. Joseph Hospital, Yonkers

Wolf stood by Bella's hospital bed looking at her, wondering if this was all his fault. He would never in a million years picture Bella shooting heroin and taking prescription pills. The doctor said she overdosed on drugs and if he didn't showed up when he did then she would have been dead. He hadn't left her side yet. She went in and out of consciousness due to the heavy meds she was on.

The doctor said she would have to enroll her into a mental center because they believed she tried to kill herself. They labeled her overdose a suicide because of the amount of prescription pills she had in her system. When the doctors told Wolf she lost her unborn seed, Wolf was sick, but he still hadn't told Bella yet because she hadn't fully woken.

Wolf sat down with a lot on his mind, but his main worry was his father, whom he never met. Hearing Aguilera say his father was a very powerful man and a hitman made him think this life was already chosen for him. Rita never talked about his father Ryan. At one point, she used to tell him he was as just as good as dead because he ran off with another bitch, just like his other brothers' and sister's father. Wolf had a lot to figure out real soon and he prayed time was on his side because he had to pay someone a special visit real soon.

Bella's eyes slowly opened, looking at Wolf. "Hey," she said in a low voice like she was in some serious pain.

"How you feel?"

"Okay, I guess. My stomach hurts. Is my baby okay in me? What the doctor say?" Bella asked, sensing something wrong because he was silent with his head down.

"I'm sorry, Bella, the baby didn't make it. You had a miscarriage," Wolf told her, watching tears roll down her cheeks.

"I'm sorry I failed you," she stated.

"It's okay, baby. This will only make us stronger, baby, but we gotta get you help."

"That was the first time I ever tried to kill myself, Romeo. I don't need help. I just need time to grieve over my father's loss."

"I know, but you still need to get some treatment, baby. You almost lost your life, baby," Wolf added, looking into her soft eyes.

"Okay, I'll do it for you, but I'm not crazy, babe. I just went through a depression phase and it got the best of me."

"Where did you get the drugs from?"

"I'm not a snitch."

"You're a cop," he told her.

"Yeah, but I don't want to talk about right now. I'm sure I'm paying my dues now," she said, feeling weak and tired, ready to go back to sleep.

"Okay, get some rest," Wolf said, tucking her in.

***

Club Express, Yonkers

The club was popping today. Niggas and bad bitches from all over came out to the newest club in Yonkers. YFN Lucci and his crew had just performed on stage, shutting shit down, and now Rich the Kid was up next. Tonight, was Two Gunz's birthday party, so the Bronx was heavy in the building. Two Gunz was a party promotor and a plug. When Two Gunz gave his time back to the court, his brother blessed him with so many bricks of coke he could have built a snow mansion. To keep his money clean, he invested his money into two clubs, one in Yonkers and one in the Bronx, and he played the background as a big club promotor. Life was good since being home, but he still kept in touch with his homies up top, especially CB. He used to always tell CB he would open a club in Y.O. because there weren't too many clubs in Yonkers. Last week CB told him, he wanted him to meet his brother Black and he agreed.

Two Gunz and Black were in the VIP section talking business and building.

"Starting next week, I got you, bro. 24 for a key is unheard of right now, my G," Two Gunz said, dripping in diamonds.

"That's what's up. Just hit me when you ready. CB talked heavy about you," Black said, sipping on Ciroc.

"That's my guy. Good nigga."

"Facts. But I'ma hit this hotel party in Brooklyn. I'll be waiting on your call," Black said, getting up to leave.

"A'ight, bro," Two Gunz said as seven of his goons walked back into the VIP section, having given him time to handle his business affairs.

"That nigga look familiar, son," Wraith said.

"Son's name is Black. He from out here."

"Oh, okay, he look like a jack boy from the BX that robbed Quan," Wraith said.

"Nah, boy getting to a bag. His bro is my homie's son, stamped. He valid," Two Gunz said, drinking Dom P.

***

Andy walked in the club with his crew of ten niggas. He saw how packed and litty it was, but there were more niggas than bitches, which Andy hated.

Andy needed to get some air because his life was crazy. After losing his pops and grandmom, he felt responsible. When he received the news of his soldiers being killed by a nigga named Lingo, he knew he had to be the one responsible for the deaths in his family. After doing his research, he found out who Lingo was, but the reason he didn't know who he was is because Lingo was from across town and he was locked up. Since he knew who he was now, he wouldn't stop at anything to find him and kill him. Smurf was going to come out, but he changed his mind at the last second.

"Andy, that's him," Lil D said, looking at the bar.

"Who?"

"Mack," Lil D said, remembering his cousin telling him Mack from Riverdale was one of the niggas who had killed his homies on Elm Street last week.

"We out," Andy said after looking towards the bar to see Mack with three other niggas, buying out the bar like they owned the place. On Andy's way out, he bumped into Black.

"Excuse me," Andy said, walking past him in a rush. He knew who he was but hadn't seen him in years.

Once outside, Andy strapped up and waited on the side of the club with his crew. No guns were allowed in the club, so Andy knew Mack and his crew were ass out tonight. Twenty minutes later, Mack stepped out of the club, but before he made it to the street, shots were fired from all directions. Mack and his crew were crawling away from the rain of bullets, but it was useless. Andy and his shooter got close to them.

"You killed my family," Andy said, standing over Mack.

"Lingo did it! I swear it wasn't me!" Mack cried.

"He next," Andy said, emptying his clip into Mack's face.

Two trucks pulled up and Andy hopped in the first Ben G-Wagon speeding off. Nobody had seen the vicious murder or heard the gunshots because the club music was so loud, until people came outside to see blood everywhere.

Chapter 7

Riverdale, Yonkers

"Oh shit, sssss," Lingo moaned, watching Ariana use her dick sucking expertise. Her thick lips meet his balls as she swallowed him whole while he slowly thrust into her warm mouth.

"I like when I suck your dick, daddy," she said, looking up at him with her bright greenish eyes that drove him crazy.

"Keep sucking, baby," he said, forcing his dick further down her throat, trying to choke her. But she wasn't going out like that. Her tongue danced around the tip of his dick then she threw him down her throat again until she felt his cum pour down her trachea.

"Damn, Ariana," he moaned thinking it was break time.

"Damn what? Nigga, you know what time it is. I'm tryna see what that mouth do," Ariana said, sitting her fine ass on his face. "Eat me, nigga," she said, feeling his tongue lick in between her tiny slit. Ariana started to grind on his face, feeling her climax climbing as her pussy juices covered his face and dripped all over the bed.

"Yessss, zaddyyyy, I'm cumminggg!" she screamed. Lingo focused on her clit while popping his finger in her pussy, going crazy while she met her orgasm. "Aaahh, ohhhhh, I need that dick now," she said, not taking no for an answer. Ariana bent over on the satin sheets, arching her back, ready to feel him in her guts.

Lingo looked at her phat, bald yellow pussy with cum pouring out. Her pussy was always tight so he short stroked inside of her walls, feeling her pussy muscles grab his dick like a firm handshake.

"Ugghhh! Fuck, babe!" she screamed when he started to ram his dick in and out, smacking her yellow cheeks, getting deeper in her guts. "You're gonna make me cum, nigga!" she said, catching another orgasm with his dick inside her pounding her walls out.

Ariana was beautiful, five feet tall, long black hair, green eyes, high yellow, nice perky B cup breasts, and a round nice ass to match her petite frame. She was tatted up from neck to feet, which made her look more exotic.

"That was worth the wait. You ain't been home all day," she said, looking at her phone, which was on vibrate, to see twenty-one calls were missed.

"I've been trying get right," he said, lying down watch her make a call.

They had been together for twelve years. She was the only person who held him down his whole bid like a trooper. Lingo knew she deserved to be treated like a queen and he was going to be the man she dreamed of.

Lingo saw her pick up the phone with tears in her eyes. He knew something serious must have happened because she never cried.

"Someone just killed my brother outside of that new club," she said sadly.

"Mack?"

"Yeah."

"Fuck!" Lingo shouted, knowing it had to be Andy's crew because Mack had no beef.

"I told him to leave that street shit alone, and now look. I'm glad you ain't go out with him, but my mom at the hospital so I'ma go," she said, getting dressed.

"I'ma come with you," Lingo said, getting dressed.

***

Yonkers, Elm Street
Days Later

It was a late night on the block and niggas were out on every corner enjoying themselves.

"How we going to get inside, bro? It's too many niggas outside. We gonna get bodied before I even step foot on the block," Trap said.

"Nigga, would you shut up!" Black shouted, looking up the block, trying to form a plan.

Since Black had seen Andy at the club, he knew he would be his next target because. Word was he had Yonkers on lock with the birds and Black wanted in. Black also wanted his block, which was Elm Street, where Black was also from. He saw fiends from all over the city coming to cop work, which he never saw before, so he knew Andy had some fire product.

"We got enough gunpower to turn this shit into 9/11?" Trap asked seriously.

"9/11 was a terrorist attack, stupid."

"You know what I mean, son."

"I got a plan. We going to cut through the next block and creep through the alley to get to his trap spot. Luckily the building is at the end of the block, so we can creep up through the fire escape," Black said.

"What if they don't have a fire escape?"

"Nigga, this Yonkers. Every building got a fire escape, fool. Come on, we out. Stop asking questions," Black said, hopping out with a Draco tucked.

Black and Trap sneaked through two back blocks until they made it into a small alley leading to one of Andy's trap houses that Black heard about.

"Shhhh," Black told Trap, who was breathing hard as they started climb the ladder until they made it to the second level.

Black looked inside the unlocked window to see someone's bedroom, which was perfect for what he had in mind. Once inside, Black led the way, listening to the loud noise coming from the living room. Black peeped around the wall to see four niggas playing a PlayStation game system with guns and gambling. Black saw the bathroom door in the hallway open and a young nigga with a blunt in his mouth step out.

"Yo, what the fuck!" he yelled until Trap quieted him with bullets.

Black turned around the corner blasting.

Tat-tat-tat-tat-tat-tat-tat-tat!

Black killed everybody in the room while Trap went to search for drugs and money. Black looked around at the dead bodies, making sure everything was cool and nobody was alive.

"Got it!" Trap said with a laundry bag in his arms.

"We gotta get out of here," Black said on his way back out the window to make a clean getaway as if he was still robbing banks. When they made it outside into alley, they ran back to the car.

***

"Yo, T-Boy, somebody just robbed us and killed J Dubb and them!" a little nigga yelled out the window to T-Boy and his crew posted on the block. After hearing gunshots, he went to check on J Dubb, who was already dead.

T-Boy was Andy's worker and cousin. He looked around to see how someone could even get upstairs, and he saw two niggas down the block with the laundry bag he used to hide drug and money. "Down there," T-Boy said, running down the block with his gun out along with twenty goons. They all started shooting at the Honda Civic pulling out, busting its windows out before it bent the corner.

T-Boy was pissed. One of the dudes looked familiar, but it was so dark out that he couldn't really see too well. But he would know Black's face from anywhere because the two used to be best friends, especially in high school.

Chapter 8

Long Island, NY

Jiménez stepped foot out of his large, beautiful palace in one of the richest areas in Long Island. The guards awaited him in the all-Black Bentley Bentayga SUV. Jiménez was on his way to the West Coast to meet with Mexican bosses above his ranking. Being the second top ranking Mexican boss on the East Coast was hard in the past year. He lost a lot of good men, especially in the war in Yonkers, which had left both of his nephews dead.

The gates to his mansion opened as he made his way to the private jet he rented from time to time.

"What the fuck?" the driver said, feeling the front tire go out. "I think we caught a flat."

"You better hope not. Are you paying for it? The tires alone are ten thousand apiece," Jiménez said while the SUV pulled over on the dark road surrounded by woods outside of the gated community.

All three goons hopped out to check the tires out to see a needle got stuck in the front tire.

"We found the issue, boss!" one of the goons shouted.

"Good. Now call a backup car. I can't miss my flight," Jiménez said.

Boom! Boom! Boom! Boom! Boom!

All three guards' bodies hit the pavement at once from the sniper in the woods.

Jiménez saw what was going on and he panicked. He called for back but before he could even get his words out, Wolf slid into the backseat with a M4 assault rifle.

"Don't look so nervous. You're only in a state of shock. It will go away soon. But I have a couple of questions and depending on how you answer them will determine if you live or not," Wolf said coldly, dressed in all black with black paint on his face.

"You have no idea what you're about to do," Jiménez stated.

"I do. Who wants me dead?" Wolf asked.

"Powerful people, and they won't stop until you are die"

"I know that, but who?"

"I don't have those answers. Maybe your life is worth more than you think."

"Why was your name in Aguilera's files?"

"Aguilera took the bounty to kill you, but I guess he used you in the meantime and let his greed get him killed. But he is only one in a million people who will be coming for your head real soon," Jiménez stated.

"Who is my father?"

"If your father wants to show his face, trust me, he will find you. To be real, there is nothing he can really do about it. You're a marked man, Wolf," Jiménez said, laughing.

Boom! Boom! Boom! Boom!

Wolf blew Jiménez's brains out, climbed out, and ran back into the woods on a small trail leading towards a highway.

***

Bronx, NY

Black watched the two-story house like a hawk. The house belonged to Two Gunz and his girlfriend. Black followed Two Gunz to the house the night he left the club after the crazy mayhem took place outside. He had decided to come on this mission alone because he didn't feel like splitting everything three ways. The money and drugs he received from Andy's trap house weren't enough for him. He needed the mother load, and from what his brother and the streets said about Two Gunz, he was going to be his meal ticket. At the club, Black was rocking him to sleep, selling him big dreams he was buying just to get him in the door.

Black hopped out of the Hellcat he had borrowed from Trap and walked into Two Gunz's backyard. It was so dark he almost tripped over the waterholes. He saw the back entrance had sliding glass doors, which were easy to break in with a flathead tool. It only took him seconds to get inside and he slowly tiptoed around the crib, checking closet and cabinets for drugs. The house was quiet, but he knew Two Gunz and his gun were inside because they never left the house. Today it was a Sunday.

Black creeped upstairs to hear moaning and groans from the hallway bathroom. This gave Black enough time to search the bedroom to his left. He searched the closet first to see racks of designer clothes everywhere. He pulled out shoeboxes to find stacks of money, but no drugs. Black checked under the bed to find two SKs, two Dracos, and one AR-15 assault rifle with a bag of mags.

When he saw a zipper on the mattress, he pulled off the sheets and unzipped the top layer of the mattress to find stacks of tan keys. Black wrapped everything inside the sheets and walked into the hallway to hear more moans. He walked into the bathroom, which was steamy and hot, to see Two Gunz fucking a big butt brown-skinned chick with dreads. She was grabbing her ankles, moaning in pleasure, while Two Gunz was pounding her shit out from behind.

"Yes, Gunz, fuck me harder!" she moaned.

Black got a hard-on watching her big titties bounce back and forth. When Black finally made eye contact with Two Gunz, who was about to bust nut, his dick went limp in her.

Bloc! Bloc! Bloc! Bloc! Block!

Black fired three shots into Two Gunz's face and two in his girlfriend's neck, leaving them both in the tub under the shower water.

Less than thirty minutes later, he was in his crib with Kartina counting money and bricks of dope. Kartina was so horny from counting all the money that she just wanted to suck dick and fuck all night, and that's what she did. She let Black fuck her in her ass for over an hour, which made her cum four times. They used toys and whips to spice shit up for the night.

Romell Tukes

Chapter 9

Yonkers, NY

Bella had just left the mental hospital after a couple of tests to see if she was mentally stable and she passed with flying colors. She was released early and called her friend Christina to come pick her up so she could stay at her crib, because Wolf had put too much stress on her.

"Hey gurl, you okay?" Christina asked, helping Bella put her items in her Toyota.

"Yeah. I just want to get some sleep."

"You need it, because you look like shit."

"Whatever, bitch. Did you get the shit?" Bella asked with wide eyes.

"Yep, it's at the house. But are you sure you ready after what happened?" Christina asked seriously, showing concern for the friend she had known since high school. Christina was a beautiful white chick with a heroin habit, but she only sniffed dope, unlike Bella, who had started shooting heroin.

"Good," Bella said, smiling. The whole time in the hospital, all she thought about was getting high again. The first time she took a hit of dope, she was hooked like pookie. Getting high took away all of her problems and stress. It was her only escape. She planned to stay away from Wolf for a while until she got her mind together because right now she wasn't a hundred percent.

"What are you going to do about your job?" Christina asked, looking at her friend, mad at herself for introducing heroin to her in the first place.

"I told them I need a vacation due to a death in the family and they told me to come back when ever Im ready."

"If you can't go cold turkey, then you will never be ready, Bella. This life isn't for you. I hate myself for becoming an addict. You're so much better than me, Bella. You have a whole life and career in front of you. This dope will make your weak."

"Thank you, T.D Jakes, now please shut the fuck up," Bella said, getting frustrated with her friend's gospel chat.

***

Bronx, NY

Flow had had just gotten done fucking his girl Kia. She was a bombshell: tall, Brazilian and Black, colorful eyes, petite, and a freak. Flow had met her in Philly two years ago selling pussy on the Southwest blocks for her pimp, who got arrested for having minors sell pussy for him. Flow brought her back to New York and showed her a luxury lifestyle she never had and now she was a classy bougie bitch.

"Where you going, baby?" Kia asked, watching him get dressed.

"To handle some business. I'll be back later, bitch," Flow said, calling her a bitch, as always.

"Okay," she replied, playing on her phone with her long-manicured nails.

Flow left his crib in the Gunhill area to meet with Black. Tonight, they were planning to send some niggas to Yonkers to open shop on Elm Street.

***

Yonkers, Elm Street
Days later

"Yo, T-Boy, what's popping?" Spice asked, walking down Elm Street with a cup of lean in his hand.

"Where you been at, nigga? You ain't get my thirty calls?" T-Boy asked, sitting on milk crates in front of a corner store with a gang of niggas looking like they were ready to kill something.

"I was in Newburgh the whole time, son. And I changed my number because the feds just hit my hood."

Spice was from Newburgh, NY, but Yonkers was his second hood. He knew everybody and everybody knew him. He sold weight in Newburgh and in Yonkers, thanks to his niggas Smurf and Andy hitting him when he came home from up north.

Spice was a tall light-skinned nigga who had a thing for white chicks because he was half-white himself. He was about getting money. At the age of twelve, he had $100,000 because his brother was a big-time dope boy until he was killed by a snitch nigga who wanted to clear his name. But paperwork don't lie.

"When you were gone, a lot of shit popped off. We was robbed on London Street,"

"By who?" Spice asked, not believing him.

"I'm not sure, but I think it was Black," T-Boy said, looking up and down the block.

"Who the fuck is that?"

"You remember CB?" T-Boy asked.

"Oh, his brother the bank robber or some shit?" Spice asked, remembering who he was now.

"Facts. Boy got us. It was dark out, but I know it was him, son. I saw him"

"So what now?"

"That's not all. The other day, a crew of niggas from outta town opened shop on Walnut around the corner, acting like they just moved into the hood, but they got crack, soft, and dope moving for the low over there. They slowing my shit up," T-Boy said, upset.

"How many over there, boy?"

"Nine or ten. They be outside at night with big guns and bitchs from outta town," T-Boy said, watching a gang of crackheads walk past his crew like they weren't even there.

"Its 10 p.m. now. They outside?"

"Yeah, they always come out at 9 p.m., son."

"A'ight. Tell everybody to strap up," Spice said, walking off to his car to grab his AK and vest.

***

Around the corner

"I'm glad we came out here, cuz this shit litty out here, bro," West said.

"Facts. This shit too easy, son. This the takeover," Roll P added, drinking a bottle of Henny, watching his niggas service fiends left and right.

They were from the Bronx, the East Tremont section where all the Crips were at. Roll P was a big homie in the Harlem Mafia Crip and he was Flow's right-hand man, so when he brought the idea of him having his own block, he was down.

He met Black, who fronted him work. He wanted a 60/40 cut, which was a big blessing. Roll P knew coming to any hood he would need a crew, manpower, and shooters, so he brought his locs.

Roll P saw a crackhead causing a big scene in the middle of the street about the dime bag of crack he had just copped being too small. Cars were stopping to watch the fiend yell and scream like a madman.

"Yooo, get that nigga outta here!" P Loc yelled, coming out of the building after hearing the commotion from inside.

While everybody was busy watching the fiend, nobody saw the four-man crew coming from each block on the intersection.

Tat-tat-tat-tat-tat-tat-tat!

Boc! Boc! Boc! Boc! Boc! Boc! Tat-tat-tat-tat-tat!

Shots were coming from everywhere as the Crips were ambushed helplessly. Roll P and P Loc shot two gunmen apiece before Spice and T-Boy put over twenty bullets into their bodies.

Chapter 10

Montrose, NY

Sanderson was on his early morning jog on a local high school track behind his house. This had been his everyday routine for over twenty years before he went to work. For the past couple of weeks, he had been so focused on trying to solve Steel's murder he hadn't gotten any sleep. All fingers pointed to Wolf in his mind, even though he had no evidence on him. He planned to make up something soon. He finished his hour of running so he walked one lap just to keep his blood flow pumping.

Lately the murder rate had been at an all-time high since last year when the MS-13 gang was beefing with the blacks. Everything was happening on Elm Street and luckily Sanderson had two snitches informing him about everything going on. The main two names he was hearing were Andy and Smurf. Sanderson's new partner was a Mexican man named Detective Gomez and he was investigating Andy and Smurf.

On his way to his pickup truck, he saw a man digging in the trash can for bottles and can with two garbage bags full of bottles. He had been seeing the same bum for days doing the same shit. Sanderson didn't feel sad for bums or the homeless because he knew everybody had a choice in life. Sanderson shook his head in disgust, placing his workout bag in the bed of his truck. He heard the homeless man say something and he turned around to see a Glock 45 pointed at his face.

"Look no further. I'm here in person, bitch nigga. You harassed my mom to get to me and now I'm here. Don't nut up now," Wolf said, looking at Sanderson's fearful look.

"You deserve a prize, young man. I had a feeling that was you. What can I say? You caught me slacking. You killed my partner?"

"Yes. I did. Y'all thought I was just going to let you and Steel put me in the hospital and not retaliate?" Wolf asked.

"Most don't."

"I'm not most."

Wolf gave Sanderson all face shots before exiting the park, feeling a weight lifted off his shoulders.

Yesterday Wolf had gone to check on Bella at the mental hospital and he was told she had been recently early discharged. Wolf was confused to hear that because she didn't come home or even tell him. When he called her phone, it was off. Wolf truly didn't know what to do. He just hoped she was safe and okay. He knew she was going through a lot due to her father's death. Wolf just wanted to be there for her even though it was his fault.

***

Nepperham Street, Yonkers

Smurf was in a store buying a box of Dutches and Hot Cheetos. Smurf was on his way to meet Andy across town. He had just touched down in Yonkers from the Bronx.

Yonkers was on fire today. Police were running down on everybody because of the murder of Officer Sanderson that morning.

"Good looking, oak," Smurf said, leaving the neighborhood store. When he stepped outside, he ran into his number one most hated enemy in Yonkers: Detective Gomez, his rival. Smurf remembered when Gomez was just a normal cop. He used to chase Smurf through Yonkers every day. Smurf used to throw bricks at his patrol car along with firecrackers when he was just a kid.

Gomez was a short, dark, Mexican with a cocky nasty attitude. He was a dirty cop known for throwing drugs on niggas to have a reason to arrest them. He was a super cop and aimed for the most arrests in the city.

"Smurf, this is a nice car. I'm sure the feds would love to see how a broke nigga could pay for a brand-new Bentley GT Continental," Gomez said, leaning on Smurf's new snow white two door Bentley that he had bought two days ago in Delaware for only $220,000 instead of $310,000, the retail price.

"Your mama got good credit, amigo," Smurf said, laughing to himself.

"Laugh now, but I'm positive you won't be when I put Sanderson's murder on you and your Elm Street crew," Gomez said seriously now face to face with Smurf.

"I never heard of Sanderson."

"I bet. But you will soon. You think all those bodies last year are unaccounted for, my friend? Oh no, I'm keeping a score board and you're running out of time," Gomez said

"Why you always so mad? Or is it just your thick-ass mustache that makes you look like that?" Smurf said.

"You got a real big mouth, nigga. I bet when I nail your ass, you won't be able to keep your mouth closed."

"That's because I'ma be busy sucking on your wife's clit like a baby bottle," Smurf said, smirking.

"Keep that energy," Gomez said, walking off.

"Ay Gomez, you shouldn't leave your car parked in the hood," Smurf said, laughing, climbing in the Bentley and pulling off.

Gomez looked around for his Challenger he left across the street, but it was gone. Somebody stole his car. He was pissed he let somebody trick him, but on this side of town, he should have knew better to leave his keys in his car.

***

Cross Country, Yonkers

Andy was waiting outside the Empire Casino, which was like a mini-Vegas in one casino.

Shit had been crazy the past couple of weeks. Andy had been trying to hunt down Lingo Loc and find Black to see why he robbed his spot and opened shop on his turf. He was waiting for Wolf to pull up along with Smurf so they could get this shit in order because he knew Black was Wolf's older brother.

He saw a black BMW i8 and a Bentley pull into the lot. Wolf and Smurf hopped out of their cars at the same time, both with stressed facial expressions.

"Damn, y'all look bad. I'ma get to the point. We have issues. Someone robbed our spot and tried to open up shop. I shut that shit down, but the person who is believed to be responsible is your brother Black," Andy told Wolf.

"What? No way. Black robs banks," Wolf stated.

"That's what I thought, but he must have found a new wave because he was spotted robbing us," Andy said.

"Damn, a'ight, let me take care of Black to see what's up. I don't think it was him, but I got it," Wolf said, wondering if his brother was onto him.

"A'ight."

"I got to handle this Gomez cop. He on to us," Smurf said.

"Gomez? He a pain in the ass, but since someone killed Sanderson, police been on one. Wolf, this shit screams your name all over it," Andy stated.

"Don't know what you talking about, but some powerful people want my head, so I'm about to turn up. I already killed Jiménez. Now I'm climbing the food chain."

"We with you bro. Facts," Smurf said before leaving.

Chapter 11

Newburgh, NY

"Yoooo, what's good, my guy? You got my money?" Spice asked, climbing off his sports bike on Liberty Street, which was one was the worst hoods in Newburgh.

"Nigga, who the fuck is you, G Money from *New Jack City*? You'll get your money when I get it," Big Shine said. He had a "6'6 wide frame from lifting weights up north for fourteen years on an attempt murder charge.

Spice was astounded and dismayed by Big Shine's whole approach because Big Shine had basically helped raise him in the game. When Big Shine came home fucked up, Spice was the only nigga to put him on his feet and he did justice for his friend, putting loot in his pocket and giving him a new Range. Big Shine was selling keys for Spice and shit was moving slow, but the reason behind that was because he stepped on the coke over six times, making it weak.

The block was litty today because a big basketball tournament was across the street. Big Shine was a big homie G-Shine Blood, so he always kept Bloods around him. Spice didn't gangbang so he didn't care for it.

"When have I ever talked to you with any bass in my voice?" Spice said calmly, walking towards Big Shine.

"What? Little nigga, you're lucky I don't take your shit, fuck nigga," Big Shine said, turning around to talk to his homies.

His homies all looked at each other because Big Shine was out when Spice was just a kid and he didn't know the grown Spice.

Spice pulled out his P89 Ruger and busted Big Shine in the back of the head, catching him off guard.

"Ahhhhh! What the fuck!" Big Shine screamed, turning around to feel that the pistol had busted his nose wide open. Big Shine was dazed when he tried to grab Spice, but Spice sidestepped him and began putting a man's pistol whip game on him in front of his crew.

Spice pistol whipped Big Shine for over ten minutes until he was dead in a pool of blood.

"Who wants this block?" Spice asked the ten Bloods standing there in shock and fear, and everybody raised their hands.

***

College Avenue, Yonkers

Trap was dressed like a fiend and his appearance was fiend status with white chapped lips, a nappy beard, a dirty face, yellow teeth, and a strong odor. Trap walked through the projects to building 51, the building all the fiends were talking about having the best shit on this side of town.

"What you need, fam?" a young nigga said, sitting in the front lobby with three older niggas in Timbs talking about who was better in rapping, Jadakiss or Styles P.

"I got a buck," Trap said, showing him the blue face hundred-dollar bill.

"Go to 4B and knock four times," the young nigga said while Trap walked past them and six other crackheads coming out the staircase with the fiend speed walk.

Trap had a small earphone in has ear connected to Black, who was parked down the block waiting for Trap to say the magic word so he could make his move with Flow.

When he got to the fourth floor, two more crackheads bypassed him with big smiles, giving him head nods, letting him know they had some fire work.

He knocked four times, scratching his neck. "4B, let's get it," Trap said in a low-pitched voice, loud enough so Black could hear.

A tall skinny kid opened the door with a pushed back hair line reaching the middle of his head. "Come on, how much you getting?" he asked Trap, letting him inside the crib "Damn, nigga, you smell like piss."

"I got a hundred," Trap said, walking inside the apartment to see three niggas bagging up crack on a big round table with guns.

"I ain't tell you to walk in there. Here, take this and get the fuck out of here," the tall kid said, handing him five big rocks in a sandwich bag tied up.

Trap made his way to the door behind the kid, but when the kid opened the door, he would wish he never did it.

Boom!

Black stepped over his dead body and fired two shots into another nigga's head while Trap put six bullets in one's chest. The last man jumped up with his gun, letting off two shots, one almost taking Trap head off, and then his gun jammed. Black shot the last nigga nine times, making his body fly across the room from the powerful shotgun bullets.

It took Trap and Black six minutes to clean the house and come out with three duffle bags full of shit.

Downstairs, Flow held four niggas at gunpoint. They were all on their stomachs on the floor with their hands over there head. "Y'all finally done?" Flow said before shooting all four men in the back of their heads.

***

Wolf watched Black and two other niggas he never saw leaving the projects in a rush with bags in their hands.

"Damn, Black," Wolf said to himself, because his brother was putting him in a fucked-up position. Not only was Black stealing his shit, but Andy's and Smurf's also.

Wolf had been following Black for two days now to see if Andy was right about his brother, and now he saw that he was. Wolf had to come up with something before this got out of hand, but what? Wolf didn't understand why he would keep robbing Andy. There were many other drug dealers in Yonkers to rob.

***

Hours later

Black had had just gotten done counting money on his new money machine while sniffing a line of coke to keep himself up.

"Baby, how we do today?" Kartina asked, coming out from the backroom in a silk Versace robe.

"We did okay. I thought you was asleep."

"I was until I heard that loud-ass money machine going to work," she said, sitting in his lap, looking at all the keys of coke on the floor, which made her smile. Kartina was a gangsta bitch raised in a gangsta household around killers, her brothers and uncles.

"Sorry, love."

"It's cool. I wanted to tell you something anyway," she said.

"What?"

"I'm pregnant again."

"Yessss!" he shouted.

"Shhhh, bae, before you wake your son up," she said, kissing his lips.

"About time! Now it's time to stack it up." he said.

She nodded her head before hitting a line of coke. Although she was pregnant, Black said nothing. Getting high was just how they lived, and her pregnancy didn't change that.

Chapter 12

Yonkers, NY

Wolf walked into his condo, coming from his mom's house across town. He was searching for Bella, but he came up empty. There wasn't any friends or family members that he knew of except her father, whom he had killed. He sat down on his couch, closing his eyes, trying to get in a quick nap before he met up with Andy little later.

When he opened his eyes, he saw an envelope on his living room glass table with his name in red on it. Wolf pulled out his gun and searched his condo because someone had been there at some point today. After doing a full search, he saw no signs of a break-in or anything to make him believe someone was still there. He opened the envelope and read the neat handwriting out loud as if someone else was there.

"Dear Romeo,

This may come as a shock to you, but I'm your father. I was never there for you but I have my reasons, which kept you safe until now. It seems like you have made some enemies all the way out here in Cali. People want you dead, so I need you to come to this address below in 48 hours. Meet me at LAX airport, but just know when you come out here you may not make it back to Yonkers."

Wolf folded the letter, sitting there in awe, shocked. He stood up and walked to his room to pack his bags so he could make the flight the next morning to L.A. All he could think about was who wanted him killed so badly. He knew whoever it was had ties to powerful Mexicans in high ranks. He wondered if his father had dealings with these men or if he was one of them. Wolf didn't trust any man, not even his father. He didn't know who to listen to or believe, but he had the mindset to play for keeps.

***

Hours later

The black BMW i8 sped into the old church parking lot. Andy was posted up on his Porsche on his phone. It was 11:42 p.m. and Andy was dressed in Polo pajamas like he had just gotten out of bed.

"What's the word, my G?" Andy said, embracing his boy.

"Same shit. Where is Smurf at?" Wolf asked.

"I believe he tryna take care of his little situation with that cop nigga who been on his body," Andy stated.

"Two dead cops in two months? The city going be on fire."

"This shit already burning up."

"I know," Wolf said, shaking his head.

"That detective nigga Smurf on was the cousin of Crazy and Ortiz. I just found out, so Smurf is on one," Andy stated.

"Damn, it's like all these Mexicans are some way related."

"Facts. I got that money for you too. One of my spots got hit again and someone killed my men," Andy said, going to his car to get something.

Wolf watched Andy's every move just in case he tried to pull something funny. Andy came out of his backseat with a bookbag to see Wolf reaching for his gun with a crazy look in his eyes.

"You good?" Andy asked, handing Wolf a bag full of money.

"Yeah, I'm okay, just fixing my belt. But I know who robbed your spot," Wolf said.

"You do?"

"You was right, bro. It was Black and two other niggas I never saw before in my life. I saw him run up in College projects," Wolf said.

"I knew it! I'ma kill them niggas, son, word to my mother," Andy said, getting hyped.

"Look, Andy, I know how the street shit goes, but can you please spare my brother? He is still blood and I will handle him as soon as I get back. Let me come up with a plan, please," Wolf asked.

Andy was in deep thought. "I'ma spare his life for you, but only for a limited amount of time, son. If he jumps out there, I'ma push his shit back. But his crew dead," Andy said seriously.

"Okay, that's fair, bro."

"Where you going?" Andy asked.

"Cali, to see who wants me dead."

"You need me to come?"

"Nah, I got it, plus I'ma hit some licks out there because I'm robbing everything moving. I'ma mail you the work to unknown addresses so we can still get rich."

"Smart. I like how you think," Andy said, smiling, rubbing his hands together.

"We may need to find new areas because it's getting hot out here in the fall season," Wolf stated.

"I got Spice in Newburgh and Big Bama in Peekskill and some niggas upstate moving shit, so we good, bro. Yonkers is only pocket change compared to other areas. I just like to see my niggas eat, feel me?" Andy said. He loved his Elm Street niggas.

"Cool. I'ma hit you when I land out there. Be safe," Wolf said.

"Likewise," Andy replied as they went different ways

"Yo...Andy?"

"Yeah?"

"Please don't kill my brother."

"Nigga, I'm a man of my word," Andy said, hopping in his Porsche and racing out of the church lot.

***

New Rochelle, NY

Andy drove back home with many things on his mind and killing Black was number one. He didn't understand why he would keep robbing his spots. Andy never had a problem with Black. He didn't even really know him. He wondered if Wolf was down with Black because he was protecting him, but Andy understood that was his brother. That didn't explain how Black knew what spots to hit unless Andy had a leak in his organization. Andy never told Wolf where his spots were but one person that did had been M.I.A. since his spots had been getting robbed and everything just hit him like a ton of bricks.

Nate was the only name racing through his mind. He was the only person outside of Smurf, T-Boy, and Spice who knew about all of his trap spots and he trusted Smurf, T-Boy, and Spice with his life. Nate had been M.I.A. for weeks, but Andy had a plan for him.

With Erica pregnant and showing, life was speeding in the fast lane. He had to find Lingo soon before he struck again.

Chapter 13

White Plains, NY

Gomez and his beautiful wife Elica were out celebrating their twentieth anniversary at a five star gourmet restaurant.

"This was an amazing night, baby," Elica said, showing her winning smile, wearing her bright red Gucci dress, which fit her petite frame perfectly.

"Twenty years strong," Gomez said, drinking a glass of red wine.

"Twenty of the best years of my whole life, so cheers to twenty more," she said, tipping his glass with hers.

Elica was a schoolteacher for eighth graders. She was pushing fifty but took good care of herself by going to the gym four times a week and eating clean. She was full-blooded Mexican, just like Gomez. They had no kids because they had busy careers.

"You looking very sexy tonight," Gomez said, looking at her big juicy breasts busting out of her dress.

"How about we go home so I can show you how much better I look naked?" she said in her sexy sweet voice.

"Well, let's get the check," Gomez said, looking for the waiter because he was horny and Elica's pussy was that good snap back that will drive any nigga crazy.

What Gomez didn't know was his wife was having affairs with other men, mainly young buff black dudes. She would sometimes get gangbanged by two or three men in the same bed they slept in. Gomez didn't fulfill her sexual needs. He was only packing three inches on a good day. She had to fake orgasms every day to make him happy.

Gomez and his wife walked outside, looking into the dark sky on the warm fall night with light winds. When they made it to Elica's red BMW X5, a man stepped out of the shadows with a gun aimed at them.

"Elica," Smurf said.

"Smurf, is that you? Oh my God, what are you doing?" Elica asked.

"What it look like? This dickhead head is your husband?" Smurf asked.

"Yes. Put the gun down," she said nervously while Gomez looked confused.

"How do you know this thug?" Gomez asked, thinking about reaching for his gun.

"Let me tell you. She was my teacher and when I got older, I started fucking her. Soon after, me and the gang started running trains on her and I must say, her pussy is off the hook," Smurf said while she was blushing, thinking about the good times she had with him and his crew.

"Is that true?" Gomez said with tears.

"Baby, you know that little dick isn't going to cut it. I needed more," she said.

"Don't call me baby. How long you been having affairs?"

"Since I met you, baby. I'm sorry, you're a good man, but you're not the type of man who can please a woman. I have to use my toys after we have sex just to catch a nut," she said from her heart, which was long overdue.

"I really don't want to hear this. I have a gun here. Who wants to die first?" Smurf said.

"Kill this dirty bitch first," Gomez said with hate in his eyes.

Boc! Boc! Boc!

Elica's body vibrated, falling to the ground with three bullets in her heart. Gomez watched her take her last breath and hocked spit in her face.

"I've been waiting for this day. I wasn't the only one fucking your wife. She been around the block a couple of times. I just wish I would have known she was your wife. I would have recorded her and did the most."

"I was fucking her mom and two sisters, so I don't feel too bad," Gomez said, staring at the barrel of his gun.

Boc! Boc! Boc! Boc! Boc!

Smurf killed the old man in the Lincoln and got the fuck outta there. Luckily the restaurant was off a highway so police would take a while to arrive.

***

Auburn Maximum Security Prison

CB worked in the education building on weekends to clean up. A couple of teachers worked on weekends, but most of them had no type of life.

The building was empty except for two female teachers and him mopping the hallways. CB slid into the janitor closet.

"Come on. We only have five minutes," a cute skinny young white, blond teacher said. She was on her knees, pulling out his dick, deep throating him with ease until he grew large in her mouth. When his dick was sloppy wet, she bent over, sliding down her grandma panties and lifting her long sunflower dress. Her pussy was a little dry and very hairy with a strong musk, but CB went to work fucking the shit out of her.

"Ummm, yesssss, I fucking love you! Fuck me with that black dick," she moaned, feeling him in her stomach tearing up her insides.

CB fucked her until her nutted inside of her twice. She climaxed four times in minutes, leaving his dick soaked in her creamy cum.

"Thank you. I'll see you Thursday. I love you so much," she said in her white girl voice, walking out of the closet sideways, about to fall over.

CB got himself together, thinking about how crazy that white bitch was. She even got his name tatted on her pelvis. CB had been fucking her for three years. She brought him in phones and drugs. She was related to most of the guards, but if they were to find out she was fucking an inmate, especially CB, the most hated, they would most likely kill him or hang him, lynching him on a noose.

CB grabbed the two iPhones and loonies under the mop bucket she had left.

***

An hour later

"What's up, young blood?" OG said in his cell, reading the noble Qur'an in Arabic.

"Same shit, OG."

"How was work?" OG asked, smiling, already knowing what he was doing down there with the cute little skinny white teacher.

"You heard what happen to Two Gunz?"

"Nah."

"His sister hollered at OBrim and told him somebody killed him and robbed him," OG said.

"Damn, that's brazy. He was doing good."

"Yeah, man, that's life. It's sad, young blood. Nobody want to see a good nigga make it. Niggas is crabs in the bucket."

"Facts. I'ma lay down until after count." CB was thinking about Black, feeling like he had something to do with his homie's death because Black was a snake nigga.

Chapter 14

Yonkers, NY

Nate was on 288, posted up in the playground with six other niggas and a couple of chicks, enjoying the Friday night. This was Nate's hood. He had run it with an iron fist for years since his cousin Art went to prison and he took over. Nate used to sell weight for Andy, his man, but he recently found his own lane and cut ties with Andy. Nate would never admit it, but he was starting to envy Andy, so Nate crossed him.

Months ago, he met Flow and Trap at his cousin's crib in the Bronx. That's where he met Black and that's when they came up with a plan to get Andy. Nate gave Black all of Andy's trap houses in Yonkers for a 25% percent cut so he could open his own block and sell weight. He thought he could trust Black after he gave him his cut from the first robbery, but he never heard from Black again. Luckily, he found a connect in Harlem so he was able to invest his money and continue to move weight in 288.

"I'ma go upstairs real quick," Nate said to his crew, passing them the blunt of loud. Nate walked into the back of his building, taking the elevator to the seventh floor where his mom lived. When he walked into the apartment, he smelled his mom's strong incense she always used.

"Mom!" he yelled, walking into living room to see his mom tied up on the floor with duct tape around her mouth, crying.

Four goons with guns stood in the living room with ice grills.

"Nate, where you been, son?" Andy asked, sitting on the couch.

"What's this about, Andy?" Nate said with a shaky voice.

"Nigga, you know what's up," T-Boy said, looking at his ex-best friend.

"I don't," he replied.

"Okay, show her to the window," Andy said as his goon dragged Nate's mom to the open living room window. They placed his mom's little body out the window, dangling her by her small ashy feet.

"Andy, don't do this. We go back, bro," Nate said, watching them hang his mom out the window.

"You got three seconds to tell me who been robbing my spots."

"Okay, just pull her in," Nate said.

"Bring that old bitch in," Andy said, staring at Nate and shaking his head because he really trusted Nate and did a lot for him over the past couple of years.

"I met Flow and Trap in the Bronx."

"Where they from?" Andy asked.

"East Tremont on Jerman Avenue."

"Okay, finish," Andy said.

"I met them at my cousin's crib and Black was there. He mentioned your name and I told him I fucked with you and I be selling weight for you," Nate said, pausing.

"Wendy Williams-ass nigga," T-Boy said.

"He said he wanted to rob you and give me a cut, then asked about someone named Wolf. He wanted to get him also, but I told him I never heard of son," Nate said, catching Andy's attention.

Andy couldn't believe Black was about to snake his own brother. Now Andy knew for a fact Wolf had nothing to do with this because he was about to become a vic himself. "Was it worth it, bro? We got history."

"I wanted more. You was spoon feeding me."

"Nah, nigga, you just got greedy and bit the hand that fed you," Andy said seriously.

"Toss her," T-Boy said once Andy gave him the head nod.

T-Boy and Andy riddled Nate's body with 223 bullets. They tossed his mom's body out the window. Her body landed on the playground cement, killing her. Screams could be heard from the playground as the woman laid flat on her back, stretched out in a pool of blood.

***

LAX, L.A.

Wolf walked through the airport in L.A., looking at all the beautiful women with their West Coast swag and warm attire. Wolf wore a Balmain outfit with Timbs. On the flight, four people asked him if he was from New York because nobody wore Timbs in Cali. Walking out of the tunnel towards the entrance, Wolf hoped his dad would pop up because he didn't leave a number, only an address in Crenshaw. Once outside, he saw a clean white and a gray two-tone Wraith with tints. Wolf saw a Mexican man who looked like he could be mixed with some more shit hop out in a Michael Kors suit.

"Romeo, I'm Ryan, your father," the man said, giving him a tight hug.

"You're Mexican," was all Wolf could say.

"What do you think you are? I'm Mexican and half-Dominican," Ryan said,

Wolf looked at Ryan's greenish eyes and good hair and could tell he was his father, but he looked young. Ryan was tall with curly hair, golden skin, a nice smile, very handsome. A person would never believe he was a vicious killer, the best in Cali for hire, but he only worked for very powerful people.

"Where we going? You going to tell me what's going on?" Wolf asked, getting inside the Wraith.

"We going to South Central. I have some good friends you will be staying with and you will be well protected. Do you gangbang?" Ryan asked, pulling out of the airport parking lot, beating rush hour.

"No."

"Good, because we're going to an East Coast Crip area," Ryan said, looking at the colors on his son's clothes to make sure it wasn't red or purple or he was good as dead.

"A'ight."

"Someone sent me a large amount of money for a hit. I'm an international hitman, but I only do work for powerful people. I got the info of my target, and my target was you, kid. I don't know who sent the money. It was deposited unknown into my account, which is very rare because everybody I do business with is face to face in person, so whoever it was didn't want to be known," Ryan said.

"How much?"

"Twenty million."

"What? Who the fuck got that kind of money?"

"You'd be surprised. But most likely the hit was sanctioned from out here and I know everybody."

"You think it was someone you work for?"

"Could be, but it could be anybody. Not a lot of people know what I do so we going down the chain of command and a lot of blood will be spilled out here."

"I'm ready," Wolf said.

"You have no choice, kid, but I like your little résumé. But you shouldn't have killed Jiménez because you only made shit worse, even though you was marked dead before you killed him. You should have waited," Ryan said honestly.

"I'm not the sitting duck type," Wolf said, looking out the window at the beautiful beaches and large palm trees.

"I live a dangerous life, Wolf. That's why I couldn't be the father I wanted to."

"I understand. We good. I didn't come out here for the sob story. I just want to handle business," Wolf said.

Chapter 15

South Central, L.A.

Wolf looked out the Wraith's window at the sign that read "Crenshaw". He had seen the hood on TV and in movies, but to see it in person was amazing, especially being from New York. It was a nice day out so people were walking up and down the strip and posted up on their porches with their crews.

"Make sure you're strapped and always with Big Loc when you come around here," Ryan said, driving down a block full of houses which looked like a ghetto suburb.

"Who is Big Loc?" Wolf asked.

Ryan pulled up in front of a small house with thirty niggas outside rocking sky blue flags and blasting rap music. Wolf saw three old school 64 Impalas on Dayton rims sitting low to the ground. There were two flat benches in the front yard and two huge pitbulls laying on the grass.

"This where you going to be chilling at for a while because nobody is coming down here. Big Loc is like a brother he will have everything you need you can trust him. He's loyal," Ryan said.

"Where you going be at?" Wolf asked. He saw over thirty guns laid out everywhere on the small property.

"I'm renting a crib in Makartor Park. It's about twenty minutes away. I'm surrounded by the MS-18 gang, so I'm good," Ryan stated, climbing out of the car.

A big nigga came out of the house smoking on a blunt. He had two bad, brown-skinned bitches by his side in miniskirts with blue flags. "OG Ryan, what's good, cuz?" Big Loc said, smiling, walking down the stairs to embrace the man who showed him the game, saved his family, and made him who he was today. Big Loc was 6'9" and 385 pounds of muscle and fat. He could have been an NFL player, but after a couple of stints in Pelican Bay and Old Folsom, his football career was over and the streets accepted him. Big Loc's father was the head of the Black Gorilla Family, which was a strong prison gang on the West Coast. His father was good friends with

Ryan, so Ryan took Big Loc under his wing. Now he was the highest-ranking East Coast Crip in L.A. and a kingpin. He had LAPD in his pocket.

"What's going on, Big Loc? I see you sticking to your diet," Ryan said, looking at his stomach sticking out of his black tee.

Wolf saw everybody wearing blue Dickies, braids, and blue Chuck Taylors with white and blue laces.

"This is him?" Big Loc looked Wolf up and down. "He don't look too much like a killer to me."

"Looks should never be judged by appearance," Ryan said with a smirk.

"Facts. But we got him. He family now, cuz. You bang, homie?" Big Loc said, looking at Wolf with his cold, dark, glossy eyes.

"Nah."

"Good. I'm Big Loc, fool. Welcome to Crenshaw. What's mines is yours, homie. We family. You got your own room in the back. Let me show you around," Big Loc said.

"Y'all behave. Wolf, I'll be back to pick you up tomorrow. I gotta make some moves. I left a gift in the closet for you, and I love you," Ryan said, not waiting for a reply and pulling off.

Wolf didn't know what to say. He was at a loss for words.

"Listen up! This Wolf. He family, so treat him like you treat your mothers," Big Loc told all the Crips outside, who all gave him dap.

Wolf walked into the crib to see niggas and bitches all over the place cooking and playing cards at the dining room table. A couple of chicks eyed Wolf, but he paid them no mind because he was still stressing about Bella. But he wasn't going to turn down some good pussy.

"You got the thots on your line already", Big Loc said, patting him on his back, almost knocking him over because he was so strong. "This is your hut - I mean room. I'm still imprisoned in the mind. Later on we roll out to a house party, so be ready, fool. I'ma warn you now, shit be going down, cuz - drivebys, walk-ups... We gangbang for real, cuz, so keep your pole. We got real beef with them Florens niggas. They just killed my little brother last month. This was his room," Big Loc said before walking off.

Wolf liked Big Loc's vibes. He seemed official. He sat on the queen-sized bed. There was a desk with a laptop to his left, a flat screen TV, blue flags everywhere, and a closet with a small window. He checked the closet to see a rack of new designer clothes, everything from Balmain, Valentino, Gucci, Fendi, off-white sheers and belts. Everything was his size. He then saw a big blue duffle bag on the floor. He dragged it out of the closet because it was too heavy to carry. He opened it to see guns of all types, from handguns to assaults rifle. There were stacks of money in rubber bands and an old picture. Wolf looked at the picture to see his mom and Ryan holding a baby in his arms, smiling in front of a mansion. Wolf knew the baby was him. He realized Ryan looked just like him when he was younger. Wolf felt a wave of emotion overcome him so he placed the pic in his pocket.

Wolf laid down, trying to take a nap, but the music was so loud. He saw a box of earplugs on the dresser, which made him laugh.

***

Cherry Valley, L.A.

Ryan parked behind a pink Maybach in the driveway of the mini mansion. Cherry Valley was a nice upper-class area where a lot of wildfires took place. He was here to visit a very important person who he knew could point him in the right direction.

As he walked up the flight of stairs, the front double doors opened. Two guards were there standing side by side, blocking the door.

"Let him in, gentlemen," a soft female voice said.

Ryan walked inside to see Marie standing on the staircase in a long silk robe, ice grilling him. Marie was a Mexican woman, tall, beautiful, and the daughter of a cartel boss in Mexico. Months ago, her father paid Ryan to kill his son. He was fucking Marie at the

71

time; unaware she was the daughter of Chico. When she found out Wolf killed her brother, she cut ties with him. She wanted to kill him, but her father begged her not to. She sold coke in L.A. and was very connected.

"Hey Marie, can we talk for a minute?"

"I should blow your brains out," she said.

"I didn't know Miguel was your brother or I wouldn't have took his job," he said.

"Come out back," she said, walking through her house. Ryan watched her ass bounce under her robe. Her ass was fake, but big and soft. He missed hitting it from the back and making her scream his name. "What?" she said, sitting in a chair next to her garden.

"I need some help. Someone wants a kid from New York dead and I need to know why?" he asked, looking into her sexy blue eyes.

"The Wolf kid who killed Jiménez?" she asked.

"Yeah, that's him."

"That's outside my pay grade, Ryan, but I'm hearing the Five Families have something to do with that," she said, seeing his eyebrows raised.

"I work for them. Why would they do that?" he said out loud, but really thinking to himself.

"They must have sent you on a dummy mission. Since when are you scared to kill anybody? But I have heard this kid is the real deal," she said seriously, crossing her thick long legs, showing her manicured pink toenails in her heels.

"So I've heard."

"I feel like you're not telling me something," she said.

"The kid is my son."

"What! You got kids?"

"Yes, one. Wolf."

"Wow," Marie said, shocked. "Someone wanted you to kill your own son? Sad. But if I was you, I'd start with Diego. He only lives blocks away from here. I hate him," she said.

"I will, thank you."

"Sure. So that's all you came for?" she said sexually.

"For now," he said, getting up to leave. He saw a glass fly past his head.

"Don't bother coming back, asshole!" she shouted, upset he didn't give her any dick.

Romell Tukes

Chapter 16

Yonkers, NY

Smurf was sucking on Namio's big double-D breasts while she rode his dick, bouncing her little butt and rolling her hips.

"Yesssss!" Namio screamed, dancing on his shaft.

Smurf spread her ass cheeks and forced himself deeper inside of her, making her go crazy. They had been fucking for hours in the hotel since they came there from the club they met at.

"I'm cumming on this big dick, ohhhh shit!" Namio yelled, cumming before her body went limp.

Smurf bent her over and fucked her from the back until he came hard inside of her gushy pussy, which was a little loose with no grip.

"Oh my God, Smurf! Your name is Smurf, right? I'm sorry I'm so fucked up," she said, lying there out of breath. Namio was a cute dark-skinned chick who wore wigs. She had big breasts, a little ass, and big dick sucking lips.

"It's Smurf, ma. How you sucked my dick for two hours and forgot my name?"

"Sometimes it be like that, right, daddy?" she said, leaning in for a kiss.

Smurf dodged the kiss by reaching for his phone on the dresser. "Tell me about me about your brother."

"What is there to talk about? He's my stepbrother and I don't fuck with him," Namio said not feeling Smurf ducking her kiss because he was kissing all over her in the club.

"Where y'all go wrong?" Smurf asked.

"You come here to fuck me or fuck my brother, nigga?"

Smurf slapped the shit out of her. "Watch your fucking mouth!" Smurf demanded.

"I'm sorry. I didn't mean it like that," she said, rubbing her face. "Now tell me more about him."

"His girlfriend Ariana think she the shit, always acts like her shit don't stank. That fucking bitch fucked my man and his brother," Namio said, getting upset thinking about Ariana.

"She a dog."

"Yep."

"Where she be at?"

"Why, you want to fuck her too?"

"Never. Only you, beautiful."

"She stay on Riverdale. I'm going to sleep now. I have to get up early for work," she said, turning around.

"I'm sorry for hitting you, but I'm into you, ma," Smurf said, sliding his finger into her loose pussy.

"You are, daddy?"

"Yeah."

"Show me," she said, cocking her legs open so he could go down on her.

Smurf looked at her like she was crazy because he never ate no other bitch's pussy expect his wifey Shantell's. But Smurf took one for the team and ate her pussy like pasta for thirty minutes straight, making her climax back-to-back.

***

Macarthur Park, Cali

In the Orcha Thai food restaurant, Ryan and Wolf walked inside to see ten Mexicans gangbangers sitting at three tables. The place was half-empty today.

"Ryan, what's up, fool?" Largo said, standing up to embrace the man he looked up to and who did a lot for him and his 18th Street homies. Largo was young with tattoos all over his face and head, tall, an MS-18 gangsta. He loved his hood. Normally their rivals were the Riders, a crazy group of Mexican gangbangers. Largo was from Makartor Park on Bonnie Brea Street next to Daman Street.

Largo's uncle was one of the first MS-18 members before he was killed by a crew called CRS in Echo Park.

"This is my son, Wolf," Ryan said, sitting down with Wolf.

"What's good, fool? Largo, MS-18."

"We got a problem, Largo, a big problem with the Five Families."

"Damn that's dangerous, fool. Them fools don't play, homie. I thought you was down with them?" Largo said, confused because the five Mexican families had control over everything from drugs to gangs and murders.

"They want my son, I believe, and I'm not having that. So you down?" Ryan asked.

"Yeah, I'm down. Who's first?"

"Diego."

"Good. Tu sabes donde el vive?   (Do you knew where he lives?)" Largo asked.

"Of course. I'm paying him a visit first thing in the morning, so be ready," Ryan said, about to leave.

"Okay," Largo said, ending the meeting.

***

Cherry Valley, L.A.

Diego laid in his bed, sleeping peacefully in his 16.2-million-dollar mansion, one of many he had in the states. Diego had been born and raised in the worst area of Usulután in El Salvador, but when he came to the States he met Cruz and became a powerful boss under Cruz. He was in his 50's and rich. He had a crew in L.A., mostly MS-13 and the Ave Boyz, moving his product, which was heroin and crystal, a.k.a. ice. He lived a crazy lifestyle, partying all night and day. Twelve goons surrounded his mansion in and out all day to make sure the boss was safe. Diego was at the lowest of families in rank, but he was still a big dawg.

The sound of gunfire woke him up out of his sleep. It sounded like a gun range outside his bedroom doors. Diego ran to his closet to grab his vest and pistol. All of his assault rifles were next door, but the only way out was to go into the hallway with the gunfire. There were sixteen rooms in the mansion. Diego know he had time to make it to his safe room down the hall. Diego was slowly opening his door when he heard the gunfire calm down.

"Where the fuck you going?" Ryan said, aiming an M4 at his face while Wolf pointed his AR-15 at him.

"Ryan? Tienes muchos guevas para venir a mi casa. Vaza pagar por esto (You have big balls coming into my home. You will pay for this)," Diego said, wondering why Ryan and Wolf were laughing at him. Diego looked down to see he only had on his Superman underwear, which was extra tight.

"Drop the gun," Wolf ordered.

Diego did as he said because he was outnumbered. "Ryan, you're making a big mistake. You know the other families will have your head."

"I know, but it's the risk I have to take. Now who paid me 20 million to kill the Wolf kid from New York?"

"My English is bad——" Ryan shot Diego in his leg. "Ahhhhh!" Diego shouted. "Okay, all I know is someone wants him dead and there paying big money. You had a timeline and since you didn't meet the time period, someone wants you dead now also. Jiménez was the icing on the cake for Wolf, whom I assume is you?" Diego said, holding pressure to his leg to stop the pain and bleeding.

"Who put the hit out?" Wolf asked.

"I don't know, but I do know they are over me," Diego said

"It's someone in the Five Families," Wolf said.

"I can't answer that. I will die in honor before I tell on my people," Diego said coldly.

"Tienes más informacion antes de que te mate con honor? (Do you have any more information before I kill you with honor?)" Ryan asked. Wolf wondered what his pops was saying because Wolf didn't speak Spanish. "Say nothing else," Ryan said, shooting Diego ten times. Wolf shot him twenty times. They walked out together, stepping over Diego's men's dead bodies to meet Largo and his crew outside twenty deep, ready to leave the crime scene.

Romell Tukes

Chapter 17

Mount Vernon, NY

"These niggas think we wasn't going to catch them with their goofy asses," Andy said, watching a brick building on 10th Street next to a corner store.

"Yeah, son got that shit jumping," Smurf said, seeing fiends in a line wrapped around the corner at 11:15 p.m.

"Facts. But I'm supposed to holler at Trigger about our next re-up and hopefully Wolf sends some weight up here from the West Coast. He supposed to hit my line soon," Andy said.

"I can't believe he in Cali putting in work, bro. That nigga on some real black hitman shit," Smurf said, texting Namio, who hadn't stopped texting or calling him since he smashed her.

"Boy be on his shit, you heard? Niggas want his head," Andy replied.

"I know. He going to be good. I got some info on Lingo and his girl Ariana."

"Ariana? That name sounds familiar. Ohhhh, that's the cute bitch I smashed a couple of years ago. I heard she was selling pussy, all types of shit."

"I don't know. But we going to take care of Lingo soon. Let's take care of this situation first. On another note, I saw that Gomez shit on the Channel 12 news and you wasn't playing. His wife looked familiar, boy."

"Oh, I forgot to tell you, that was Elica, the old head Spanish bitch we all had in the spot for four days passing her around."

"Damn, her pussy was fire too. I remember her," Andy said, thinking back.

"That shit starting to clear up, son. Let's handle this shit," Smurf said, pulling out his 9mm Glock with a 30-round clip.

Andy and Smurf made their way to the building to see a brown chick come out with big eyes, an awkward face, and a huge ass they saw from the front.

"Damn," Smurf said, looking at the crackhead's ass jiggling everywhere.

"Bro, she look like a mental health patient."

"Yeah, with a phat ass," Smurf added.

"This is it," Andy said, standing outside of apartment 1-D

"Knock, nigga."

"Nigga, you knock. I always knock," Andy replied as a fiend opened the door to come out.

Andy shot the fiend in his chest, kicking him to the ground and rushing the crib. Andy had heard about the shit from a chick who used to fuck Black and still kept in touch whenever he needed a booty call.

Boc! Boc! Boc! Boc! Boc!

Smurf killed the fat nigga in the kitchen while Andy hit the nigga at the dining room table counting money.

"Ahhh, shitttt!" the nigga with the bald head and goatee said, sitting down in pain after Andy shot him in the shoulder.

"Who you work——"

"Black and Flow," the dude said, finishing Andy's sentence.

"Where can I find them?" Andy asked.

"I don't really know, but Black be around White Plains Road, bro. I just sell for them. Please get me some help. I feel dizzy."

"That won't be needed," Smurf said, shooting him once in his large eye.

"Bullseye. You want this shit?" Andy asked, looking at the money on the table.

"Hell nah, I'm rich now, nigga. This ain't back in the day," Smurf said, following Andy outside so they could hit Black's other spot.

***

Westwood, California

Sousa stared out his private silent room window, where he always came to clear his mind and meditate. This morning he received the news about Diego's death and he was upset about it because

Diego was a trustworthy member of their organization and the Five Families.

A maid who was hidden in the closet at Diego's mansion told Sousa what happened and who she saw. When she mentioned Ryan's name, Sousa already knew what it was about: the bounty on his head.

Sousa knew Ryan very well. The two were close and had a strong respect for each other. He knew Ryan was nobody to be taken lightly. Word was Ryan had over 200 bodies. He did a lot of work for cartel families and Black Hands in L.A. and the Five Families that ran the West Coast.

Sousa had been born in Aguascalientes, Mexico around a vicious cartel family, but when he moved to Cali, he met Ruiz and Cruz. When he met the two brothers, his life changed and he became a part of the families. Sousa was also a Black Hand with a crew of MS-13 ready to go for him at any moment. Everywhere Sousa went, he traveled like the President of the United States. Sousa had put a hit on Ryan this morning. Now he had two bounties on his head and his goons were ready to hunt.

"You okay, papi?" Sousa's wife walked into his private room. No one was allowed in except her.

"I'm doing well, love. Thanks for asking. Where are you going?" he asked, seeing her dressed in a dress and heels.

"Shopping, nails done, and spa." Julie was breathtaking. She was thirty years old, short, curvy, sexy, with a flat stomach, thin waist, long black hair, and nice thin lips. She was Mexican and Honduran. She used to model back home in Honduras until someone killed her father and mother over money. When she came to the States at the age of eighteen, she met Sousa and married him. Sousa was ugly, fat, and out of shape, but he took good care of her.

"Okay, roll with security because Diego was killed this morning and until we find out what's going on, I want you to be safe," he said, standing up to kiss her.

"Okay, papi," she said, leaving, swaying her hips.

Sousa looked at the plump ass he loved to eat every night. He even let her piss and shit on him. He was into some sick shit, but she met his demands.

***

Beverly Center Mall, Cali

Wolf was going shopping for some clothes. He spent two hours in the mall while two Yukon trucks full of Crips waited for him in the garage next to the new White Audi S8 sedan he copped two days ago. On his way out the Louis Vuitton store, he dropped two bags because he couldn't carry any more. He already had ten bags on his arms.

"Let me help you," a female voice said, squatting down in a dress and heels to help him. Wolf saw her sexy toes and legs and then slowly looked at her face to make eye contact. They both were struck by each other and at a loss for words.

"Thank you. I'm…uhhhhh…" Wolf said, forgetting his name while she laughed. "Sorry, I'm Romeo."

"Nice name. I'm Paola."

"Thanks, but I got it."

"No, let me help. Are you leaving?"

"Yes."

"Me too. I got you," she said, showing her Colgate smile and colorful eyes.

Wolf looked at her breasts and ass. She was stacked up nice in all areas. She was catching everybody's attention. Paola was 100% Mexican with a yellow complexion, goldish hair color, deep dimples, C-cup breasts, and piercings in her dimples and lips. She was a trophy.

"You must live around here."

"Damn, it's that obvious?" she said, laughing, looking at her ladies Rolex watch.

"No, just asking because I'm not from out here."

"I'm from Mexico originally, but I been out here since I was an infant. Where are you from? Hold on, don't tell me… New York," she said, looking at his Dior sweatsuit and Balenciaga sneakers. West Coast niggas weren't heavy on high fashion designer clothes like East Coast dudes.

"It obvious?" he said, walking into the garage.

"Yeah, your outfit, but you look cute."

"You're beautiful," he said as one of the Crips blew the horn so he'd hurry up.

"That's your crew? You roll deep. Are you in a gang or something?" she asked, seeing blue flags in the Yukon window mirrors in both trucks.

"Hell nah. But where is your car?"

"Next to the Audi I almost hit. He would have been mad. I hate driving," she said, seeing him hit the push to start button on the keychain to the Audi. "My bad."

"It's cool. I wouldn't have minded. Thanks for the help. Can I have your number so you can show me around?" Wolf said.

"Yeah," she said, telling him her number after he put his bags in his car.

Wolf helped her inside of her Mercedes Benz CLA 250 while the Crips called him a lover boy and told him to hurry up.

Romell Tukes

Chapter 18

East L.A.

Som Club was a ghetto strip club in East L.A. in the hood. The small club was dark and filled with big booty dancers everywhere trying to make a couple of dollars to feed their kids or pay for their college tuition.

"This shit ain't as ghetto as I thought it would be from the outside," Wolf said to Big Loc. They were their own section, surrounded by a mob of Crips.

"Nigga, this ain't New York. We ain't got Sue's or Club Angels down here, homie. I used to see that shit in them *Phat Puffs* mags. I always wanted to make a trip down there," Big Loc said, drinking lean out of a cup.

"You mean up there," Wolf said, correcting him. Big Loc gave him the evil eye because he didn't like to be corrected.

"Yo, cuz, y'all niggas go enjoy yourself. Ain't no ops in here, fool," Big Loc told his goons posted up on the wall. When they left, Big Loc called two of the baddest dancers in the building to come entertain them.

Wolf enjoyed himself, getting ten dances and bagging four strippers who were on his body. They all left the club before 11 p.m., heading to the after party in Compton at Big Loc's cousin's house, who was a Compton Crip.

Wolf didn't drink, so he was always on point at all times. When he saw the old school Chevy Cutlass creeping up the block with its light off, he went into action.

Bloc! Bloc! Bloc! Bloc! Bloc! Bloc! Bloc! Bloc! Bloc!

Tat-tat-tat-tat-tat-tat!

Wolf killed the driver and passenger, but the Mexican in the backseat killed two Crips before Big Loc and four other Crips lit his ass up with bullets. Everybody hopped in their cars, speeding off.

"You was on point, cuz. You saved our lives, cuz. You got some skills. I had doubts, but I guess you really are your father's son," Big Loc said.

"Yeah, who was that anyway? They were Mexicans?"

"Either they were our rivals the Florens or niggas coming for you. Same shit," Big Loc said, driving into Compton ten cars deep, ready to turn up in a house party.

Wolf saw how the block was flooded with low riders and blue flags everywhere. Wolf was overwhelmed by shit. It was too much.

***

Riverdale, Yonkers

"Uggghh, fuck! Ummm," Ariana moaned with her legs spread wide open in the air while Lingo long dicked her, making her go crazy.

Lingo felt himself about to bust, but he held back and he dove deeper in her waterfall as her pussy walls clenched on his dick.

"Yessssss!" she screamed, biting her lips, digging her nails into his muscular back. She thrust her hips into his while he pounded away.

Lingo caught a cramp in his thigh while they both hit their climax. Lingo jumped out of her creamy pussy. "Shit!" he shouted, shaking his leg, trying to get the cramp out.

"You okay, baby?" she said, laughing, putting on her panties and getting dressed so she could go to her little cousin's crib to help her babysit.

"Yeah. What you doing this morning, love?" he asked, sitting down, admiring her sexy curves and phat ass.

"Gotta go help Lisa with her baby. She so young, baby. I can't believe she let that old dust head nigga get her pregnant. She only sixteen and he in his thirties," Ariana said, putting on her Chanel jeans that made her ass sit up right.

"I got go to Queens. I'ma call you later," Lingo said, now dressed, grabbing his keys to leave.

***

Ariana drove down Elm Street to her cousin's house, which was a couple of blocks away. She hated coming over here to this side of town because she did a lot of dirt when Lingo was gone and prayed it never got back to him. When Lingo was gone, Ariana had no plans on being loyal for no damn ten years. She was young and full of cum. She held him down with visits, money, pics, mags, tapes, 35 pounds of food a month, and whatever else he desired. Her whole thing was to never let shit get back to him because she didn't want to hurt him or what they had.

She stopped at a red light on a hill and texted her little cousin that she was near.

Boc! Boc! Boc! Boc! Boc! Boc! Boc! Boc! Boc!

Ariana caught three head shots and her upper body was riddled with bullets. Her head slammed into her horn. Andy ran down the block into one of his little homies' cribs as police and sirens flooded Elm Street in minutes.

***

Beverly Hills, Cali

Paola was in her pool going for a swim, getting a good exercise as she did daily. Paola had her own mansion, 18,171 square feet, worth 8.7 million dollars. It was a European French stone building. Nine bedrooms, six bedrooms, cathedral ceilings, a private roof deck, a big gazebo in the backyard, white marble floors, and six car garages. Her brother lived there too, but he was normally in South Central with his gang. Mario was only nineteen and heavy into the streets when he didn't need to be because they were well taken care of, thanks to their wealthy mother.

Paola was twenty-four years old and her head was on straight. She had graduated from UCLA with a law degree two years ago. She was smart and beautiful, a double threat.

She had thought about Wolf since she met him last week, wondering why he didn't call. She was single, but she didn't date. For some reason, Wolf had her panties dripping wet since she first laid eyes on him.

Chapter 19

Bronx, NY

Black and Flow were on Fordham Road shopping area, grabbing some gear from a couple of designer stores.

"What's up with your people in Soundview? They ready for us to open shop?" Black asked, looking at a pair of Valentino shoes.

"Yeah, son, that's a go, boy. We litty over there and I'm tryna holler at Wheely from Weeks Avenue to see if we can set up some shit over there," Flow said.

"Good. We gotta spread our wings, especially after this bitch ass nigga robbed our spot."

"Facts."

"They did your boy dirty a couple of weeks ago," Black said, shaking his head.

"I saw it on the news when I was in the crib. They tossed his mom out the window, bro. That was some real OG Mafia you-owe-me-money type shit," Flow stated, looking at a shawty who was smiling at him and winking.

"Them niggas just slumped a bitch on the hill on Elm yesterday," Black said.

"Do you think it was a good idea going against them niggas?"

"Fuck them. Shit, they got us to where we need to be, right?"

"Them niggas killed P-Loc and all them niggas, bro. They been putting it down out here, bro. A lot of niggas is sick about that," Flow stated.

"That's life," Black said, leaving the store.

***

Andy came out of a jewelry store on Fordham Road to pick up a necklace for Erica, who was due in a month or so. She was showing a lot. The baby shower was two days ago.

Since killing Ariana, he had been laying low. Her death was big, but nobody saw a thing, and whoever did was too scared to say something.

Walking down a side block to where he parked his Benz he saw Black and Flow about to climb into a GMC truck.

"Oh no," Andy said to himself, pulling out his weapon.

Bloc! Bloc! Bloc! Bloc! Bloc! Bloc!

He caught Flow in his shoulder. Black fired back while taking cover. Flow hopped in the driver's seat as Black and Andy went bullet for bullet, hitting four civilians, killing two of them. Andy ducked the bullets and fired six more shots at Black before he jumped in the truck and pulled off.

Andy ran to his Benz and dashed down the street, passing a crowd of civilians standing over dead bodies.

***

El Monte, Cali

Ryan and Wolf were on their way to meet with a good friend of Ryan's and a very connected man. Ryan needed more answers because what he had wasn't enough. Killing Diego was the talk of the town and now he was a wanted man just like his son, but he didn't give a fuck.

"How's your brothers?" Ryan asked, turning down the old Snoop Dogg album. He was Ryan's favorite rapper. Since Ryan moved to the west coast over twenty years ago from New York, his whole style changed. It was a mixture of the East and West.

"They good. CB in prison still, but I think he should be seeing the parole board soon," Wolf said, looking at the beautiful city of El Monte.

"How about Black? He still robbing them damn banks? That boy needs to find a new job. He is brilliant when it comes to them computers."

"I know. He could have went to ITC Tech. They wanted him bad," Wolf replied thinking about how Black went from robbing banks to robbing him and his crew. He spoke to Andy last night and he told Wolf it was getting nasty out there and he read between the lines.

"I'm sorry to hear about Victoria. I never got a chance to meet her because after me and your mom split, it was over. I was putting all of your lives in jeopardy. But you turned out good," Ryan said, feeling proud to be his father.

"Thanks. Do you know we're being followed?"

"Yep, for eight minutes," Ryan said, nonchalantly driving past a shopping center. "When we turn the corner, I will slow down and we gonna jump out busting. Grab them two Dracos from under your seat, son," Ryan said, seeing the minivan at least twenty feet behind him.

"Here," Wolf said, passing him the heavy Draco.

"On five. 1, 2, 3, 4…5!"

Ryan and Wolf both jumped out, shooting up the van while the Wraith was moving at a slow pace. The Mexicans in the Wraith didn't believe Ryan got the drop on them that fast.

Tat-tat-tat-tat-tat-tat-tat-tat!

When all five men were dead in the van, Ryan and Wolf jumped back in the moving car, racing off to their destination.

"You want some ice cream? I've been fiending for that for a week now," Ryan said.

"I'm down."

"Big Loc told me what happened. He said he needs to keep you around."

"He cool."

"He supposed to be protecting you, but you protecting his fat ass," Ryan said, laughing, pulling into a candy and ice cream store lot.

"I don't mind. I like living over there. It's a party every night, but I also hear drivebys and shootings every night. I never saw police come through yet to see what was going on. If this was New

York, police would have been on everything," Wolf said, walking into the store.

"Police too scared son. Last year, seven officers died in the same week, so now they let the gangs control the hood," Ryan said, making a waffle cone ice cream, adding a variety of ice creams sprinkles and candy.

***

Ossining, NY
Days Later

Lingo had just gotten done watching Ariana get buried next to her brother. Yonkers graveyards had been full for the past couple of months so they had been burying niggas in Ossining or Peekskill. The day he got the call about Ariana's death on Elm Street, he already knew what it was about. He tried to keep Ariana out of his street dealings. He wished she would have told him she was driving through Elm Street. He would have detoured her elsewhere. Lingo had nothing left in life to live for. He felt death knocking at his door. He was ready to go all out and risk his life to kill Andy and his crew.

Chapter 20

Hollywood, Cali

Dario was in his mansion on the Hollywood hills, on a video conference with Sousa for over an hour in his office.

"How come I didn't see you at Diego's funeral? You should have got your last words in. I know how close the two of you were," Sousa said on the large screen.

"Over thirty years. That's why I couldn't bring myself to see him in a casket. He was the godfather to my children. They are more hurt than me," Dario said sadly, unbuttoning the top button on his Tom Ford Suit.

Dario had been born in Mexico City, Mexico, but raised in L.A. His uncle was a powerful rich man, best friends with Ruiz, the boss of all bosses. His uncle showed him the game, and it didn't take long for Dario to climb his way to the top and become a member of the Five Families. He was in his sixties, medium height, bald head, goatee, and a scar on his face from when he was a kid. Dario and Diego were like brothers. The two were the closest in the families besides Cruz and Ruiz, but that's because they really were brothers.

"I sent some goons to go handle Ryan, but it went very wrong. I thought he was one of us, or that at least he would have enough respect for Ruiz not to cross us like this," Sousa stated, drinking on the other side of the screen.

"Es Dominicano y Mexicano, pero no es 100% Mexicano para que nunca pueda ser uno de nosotros(He's Dominican and Mexican but he's not full-blooded Mexican so he can never be one of us)," Dario said in pain, thinking about what Ryan did to his friend. Ryan put in a lot of work for Dario over the years so the two had a good rapport.

"Es muy peligroso. Tengan cuidado. Es el major asesino en la costa oeste. Todos los Manos Negros le confiaron sus vidas y familias. (He is a very dangerous man beware he is the best assassin on the West coast. Every Black Hand trusted him with their lives and families)," Sousa said.

"I don't give a damn. I got a little special surprise for him," Dario stated.

"Oh yeah?"

"Yep. He lives around the Ramp Park area and I have the whole police office on the payroll. You know they're the worst cops in Cali, so I paid them a little extra to take care of our dirty work. I also hear he has company with him."

"The more the merrier," Sousa replied.

"I have to go. I will be waiting on you within days before our family meeting. I have to go meet Cruz today," Dario said.

"Okay," Sousa said before hanging up.

***

Macarthur Park, Cali

Ryan and Wolf had just left Ryan's crib, on their way to South Central. They drove through 6th Street to see hookers and drug dealers packed in the streets. This neighborhood was mainly Mexicans and Central Americans living in the area full of buildings and a trap house on every block. Ryan loved it here because of his close relationship with the MS-18 who ran the hood. It was home to him.

"We got some leads on Dario's location, so I plan to pay him a visit soon."

"We," Wolf said, correcting his dad.

"Facts. But it's too late to bust a move now. We have everything set for tomorrow. Who is the chick you be Facetiming? You gotta watch these Cali chicks. They may look good, act classy, and sound like a good girl, but will snake you so good you won't even feel the venom," Ryan said, turning down the ramp leading to the highway.

"Sounds like you been through it before?"

"You have no clue. But when a bitch pussy is so good and you keep going back, you just learn how to deal with the venom," Ryan said, laughing.

"Looks like we got company," Wolf said, looking into the rearview mirror to see flashing lights.

"Shit," Ryan said, pulling over.

"The guns in the stash spots?"

"It's not that, Wolf. These are crooked, dirty police. They got their own gang called Ramp Park Force Gangstas."

Wolf wanted to laugh, but he saw how serious his dad's face was. Ryan knew something wasn't right the way the police car was sitting there. Ryan also knew the Ramp Park Police worked for Dario and his family.

"Grab the guns and take one."

"What?"

"Just do it," Ryan said, seeing two cops get out of the police car.

Wolf grabbed both of the Glocks and cocked it back, placing it under his thigh to conceal it as Ryan did the same.

"Ryan, get the fuck out! You and whoever you have in the passenger seat," one of the cops said, sitting ten feet away from their car.

Ryan and Wolf opened the doors to get out "Officer, I see you forgot your body cam. What type of traffic stop is this?"

"Ryan, we all know about the large amount of money that's on your head, so we came to collect," one of the cops said, reaching for his gun, but he was too slow.

Ryan shot the cop four times in his head before he even got ahold of his gun. Wolf followed up by shooting the other cop in the face twice, killing him. They left the two cops dead as they hopped in the Wraith, speeding down the highway.

"They were going to kill us?" Wolf asked.

"Shit, that would have been too easy. They would have killed us and beheaded us and taken taking our heads back to Dario for the bounty," Ryan said, knowing how the Ramp Park PD got down.

"Damn, close call."

"Yeah. They had the car camera off, their body cam lights was off...they was going do us good," Ryan said, driving towards a South-Central exit.

Romell Tukes

Chapter 21

Riverdale, Yonkers

Shantell was in a 24/7 laundromat drying the four loads of clothes she just took out the washer machine. It was 12:30 a.m. so the place was empty besides a cute black dude with dreads sitting near the candy machine washing clothing and reading a *XXL* magazine. She wore a pair of Fendi pajamas because all of her clothes were dirty and her building didn't have a laundromat so she had to come out here to Yonkers.

Smurf was out somewhere - she didn't know or care where. She was starting to get fed up with the way he was treating her. She had been finding bitches' photos in his phone, texts, sex texts, and last week one of Smurf's bitchs had the nerve to come to her crib talking about how he got her pregnant. Shantell was two seconds from beating the seed out of her to end her worries, but she didn't. She didn't even say shit to Smurf. After everything she did for him, she felt like shit. She wasn't a tit for tat type bitch, so she was going to pack up and leave.

"Excuse me, do you have change for a twenty? The machine is broke," the brown-skinned man said, smiling, looking at how beautiful she was.

"Sure, handsome," she said, flirting, thinking it was time for some new dick anyway.

"What's your name, beautiful?"

"Shantell. What's yours?" she asked, looking at his big muscles poking out of his designer shirt.

"Grim," he replied.

"Grim?" she asked with a chuckle, never hearing this type of nickname. "What's your real name?

"Reaper."

"Grim Reaper?" she said to herself before she saw the big gun in the man's hand raise to her forehead. She begged for her life. "Please!"

"Shhhh! Too bad, beautiful. There is no saving you," Lingo said.

"I've done nothing! Your beef must be with Smurf, not me!" she cried.

"Wrong. If you suck his dick, then my beef is with you also," Lingo said.

"But——"

"Shhh!"

Lingo saw her body drop after he put a hole in her head the size of a baseball. Lingo placed her body in one of the dryers before leaving.

***

Hollywood, Cali

"How many is out there?" Wolf asked from the driver's seat of an old Benz, parked across the street from Dario's mansion early in the morning.

"It looks like three, but I believe there's double inside. Dario is always well-protected. But this should be light work for you, as you kids say in New York," Ryan said.

"No, pops, nobody says that no more. I hope this works," Wolf was dressed in a mailman's uniform with a postal service hat and packages.

"Why wouldn't it?"

"Because nobody gets mail at 7:37 a.m.," Wolf replied.

"Just say the mail is backed up so you're delivering early." Ryan looked at the three men in suits in the front of the beautiful glass mansion with the nice manicured grass.

"Okay, here goes nothing," Wolf said, walking across the street halfway down the block and into Dario's long driveway.

The guards stopped the mailman, checking their fake Rolex watches.

"It's a little early for mail, ain't it?" the biggest guard asked, standing in front of Wolf, looking at the package in his hand.

"Yes, but we're backed up at the postal office due to the postal mail voting for this year," Wolf said.

"Oh yeah, that's right. It's November. We need a new President," another guard stated.

"I agree," Wolf said.

"A'ight, what you got there?" the big guard asked, watching Wolf open the box.

Wolf pulled out a Colt 45 handgun with a silencer and shot all three guards back-to-back. Ryan ran onto the lawn, entering the front door to see guards sitting in the living room watching a Mexican show. Ryan and Wolf shot five guards but were unaware of the two guards coming down the stairs.

Boc! Boc! Boc!

One of the guards hit Ryan in his shoulder, but Wolf caught both of the guards in their chests with seven shots apiece, watching them choke on their own blood.

"You check the crib for money and drugs. I'ma go find our friends," Ryan said, walking off.

Wolf went upstairs, searching every room for money and drug. Once he checked the last room, he found stacks of white bricks and money up to four feet high in the back of a closet. Wolf saw no bags, so he used the bed sheets. He tossed everything in the middle of the sheet and tied it up.

Ryan made his way into the basement to see a full gym and a bar. Farther down the hall, the basement was a house itself. Walking into the gym, he saw a shower, so he made his way in there, smelling a sweaty, musky odor. Ryan walked further into the shower room to see an indoor pool area and a sauna. Ryan saw a male figure inside the sauna room in a robe with headphones in his ear. He opened the glass door, walking through the foggy steam to see Dario with his eyes closed, Ryan slapped Dario with his pistol, scaring the shit out of him.

"Ryan, what the fuck! Come on, it doesn't have to be like this!" Dario cried watch his hand movements.

"It does."

"How did you get in?" Dario asked, wondering if his guards were still alive so they could save him.

"They're dead, Dario. Now who wants my son dead?"

"Your son?" Dario asked, confused, rubbing his swollen face.

"Yeah, the Wolf kid who killed Jiménez?" Ryan asked.

"Ryan, I have no clue about that. I heard about it from Sousa. Maybe he can enlighten you more. He also put the bounty on your head. I had nothing to do with that. We have a good relationship. You're like family to me, Ryan."

"So, I guess you're not the one who sent the Ramp Park Police after me?"

"The who? Noooo...that was Sousa. I will never cross you. I was glad when you killed Diego. He deserved it. He fucked my wife ten years ago. He is lucky I ain't kill him myself."

"Dario, you're full of shit, but I have to go," Ryan said, turning to leave.

"So, me and you good?" Dario asked nervously.

"Oh, how can I forget?"

PSST! PSST! PSST!

Ryan walked out of the sauna in sweats to see Wolf walking around looking lost.

"You ready?"

"Yeah. Any news?" Wolf asked.

"Nope, but I think I may have a clue who we can go see next," Ryan said, walking upstairs to see a bundled sheet full of money and drugs.

"If we get pulled over, don't stop. With all that shit, we'll both never see daylight," Ryan said, watching Wolf drag the heavy load outside to the Benz.

Chapter 22

Yonkers, NY

Bella laid in bed, sore and tried from the long crazy night she and Christina had in Rockland County. Money was low for both women so they went to Nyack in Rockland County and met some drug dealers who wanted to have a good time in exchange for getting high. Bella had so many dicks in her last night she lost count, but it was worth it for the high. She never did anything like she did last night. She felt disgusted with herself, but her addiction was taking control of her life. Every day she thought about Wolf, but she knew he didn't deserve her. He was too good of a man. She felt like she was damaged goods now and Wolf deserved better.

She wanted to change so badly, but it was hard to change at a time when all she could think about was drugs. Her body was in so much pain because she was dope sick. Bella went in her purse and pulled out two bags of heroin and prepared her needle for her wake-up hit.

With two bags of dope left, she knew she had to come up with a plan to get some more soon.

***

L.A., Cali
Staples Center

"That was a good game, cuz. You don't like the Lakers, fool?" Big Loc asked Wolf as they left a basketball game at the Staples Center.

"Hell nah. I'm a Brooklyn Nets fan, son," Wolf said proudly, loving all his New York teams.

"Don't say that too loud. Niggas might leave you out here, cuz," Big Loc said, making his way through the parking lot with his five-man crew.

Wolf had been having a good time in Cali, hitting up every big party with Big Loc, who knew everybody who was somebody. He had recently gone to Universal Studios, Studio City, the theater, nice restaurants, and clothing stores. He went to Six Flags with Paola yesterday, which was amazing because the two got to know each other.

Wolf wasn't a baseball fan, but Ryan took him to Dodger's Stadium in Griffith Park, which was a lifetime experience.

"What time is that flyer party, cuz?" one of the Crips asked, walking behind Big Loc.

"I think around 11 p.m. around Nickle Gardens," Big Loc said.

"What's a flyer party?"

"A big party inside of a big storage room where we can get on groove on at, cuz," Big Loc said.

Wolf saw a van door slide open and a gang of Mexicans hopped out. "Look out!" Wolf yelled before shots started to ring out.

Wolf took out two Mexicans and the Crips killed three, but everybody was unaware of the backup van parked in the cut.

Tat-tat-tat-tat-tat-tat-tat-tat!

Wolf saw Big Loc and two Crips go down and he went crazy, hitting three Mexicans in the chest. With two Crips left, the finished the job, but when they saw security guards coming their way, they let off a few shoots and took off, leaving Big Loc dead on the hot pavement next to his little homies with a gun in hand.

***

St. Joseph Hospital, Yonkers

Erica had just given birth to a beautiful baby girl weighing 7 ½ pounds and healthy.

Andy was overwhelmed holding his little baby in his hands, rocking her slowly, putting her back to sleep while Erica laid in bed drained after eight hours of labor.

"You two look so cute together," Erica said, smiling. "Now it's time you put a ring on it," she said, waving her fingers at him.

"You been drinking too much lemonade."

"Try Red Bull dealing with you."

"Whatever. I gotta step out. I'll be back in two hours."

"Ummm, gotta check in with one of your bitches?" Erica said with a jealous tone.

"No, gotta handle some business."

"You know with most men, after having kids they slow down, not speed up," she said, taking her little baby from him so he could leave.

"I'm sorry, but I'm coming back. Love you," he said, leaving.

Andy had received a shipment from Wolf out in Cali and he was about to meet Spice and Force to bust down the keys. He was going to put Smurf's work to the side, but he couldn't reach him. His phone was off, just like T-Boy's.

***

Calabasas, Cali

Cruz rode in the backseat of his stretched Rolls Royce limousine on his way home to his beautiful home in the rich Calabasas area. Crus was a part of the Five Families. He and his brother Ruiz, who was serving a life sentence in San Quentin, had started the Five Families when they were kids fresh from Mexico. He was a drug lord, rich, and connected to lots of heavy hitters across the world. The Five Families were considered a cartel family within its own organization.

At fifty-seven years old, Cruz had a head full of grays and he wore Cartier glasses to see because his vision was slowly leaving. He was an alcoholic after three divorces for assaulting his wives. He now lived a playboy lifestyle.

The only thing on his mind was losing two important members of the Five Families back-to-back, which was upsetting. Ryan was a close friend of Cruz and Ruiz. They both considered Ryan family. Now he was their target - or at least his, because he hadn't spoken to Ruiz yet. Cruz knew he had to come up with a plan quickly because when Ryan was on a mission, there was no stopping him.

Chapter 23

Rodeo Drive, L.A.

Wolf took Paola out on a lunch date. This was their second date and the vibe was crazy. They were outside eating at a nice Central American food restaurant.

"I been living out here forever and I never been here," Paola said, eating some type of seafood dish.

"I saw it a couple of days ago and I had to come here. Thanks for coming," he said, looking into her sexy eyes.

Whenever he came around Paola, he didn't even think about Bella. She was like a ghost. He liked everything about Paola and he knew there was so much more to know about her.

"So tell me more about your life and family."

"My mom is a big-time director, just like her father was before cancer took him. Me and my brother live together but he's normally in L.A.," she said softly.

"Oh, okay. What's your goals?"

"I always wanted to be an actress, but that's one in a million out here. I moved to Cali just to become an actress or model and most of them look better than me, so yeah," she said sadly.

"I doubt that, ma. You're killing every chick I seen out here."

"Don't try to gas me up with that New York swag," she said, laughing.

"I'm serious. Any man would love to put you on his highest shelf. You're a queen on her own throne, ma," Wolf said, making her blush extra hard.

"You're so sweet. How come you're not taken? You're cute, got a bag, and respectful. Are you gay?" she asked seriously.

"No, I'm not gay. I was in a relationship, but things just didn't work out."

"Oh, okay, I'm sorry to hear that. You got me now and I'm not going nowhere," she said.

"Good."

"I have a question. Why are you all the way in Cali?"

"To be honest, I recently just met my father so we been getting to know each other," Wolf stated.

"Awwwwww, that's so cool! I love to see things that."

"What you doing this weekend?"

"I was going to ask you if you want to come on my mom's yacht with me to spend so time together?" she asked.

"Hell yeah!" he said.

"That don't mean you getting none of this yummy," she said, laughing.

***

Bronx, NY

Smurf and T-Boy had been on a three-day stake out trying to catch up with Black, but the way he moved was like a snake in the nightfall.

"Yo son, word to my mother, I'm sick of this waiting shit. Let's go get this little nigga, bro," T-Boy said, looking out the tints of the BMW X5 parked outside of a daycare center, watching a group of kids play in the playground in the front yard.

"That's what you want to do? Let's go," Smurf said, hopping out with pistol in hand, crossing the street with red eyes.

Boc! Boc! Boc! Boc! Boc ! Boc! Boc! Boc! Boc!

Smurf shot three of the children. One of them was Joshua, Black and Kartina's three-year-old son, one week shy of the fourth birthday he would never see now.

Smurf walked back to the BMW and raced off with T-Boy in the driver's seat looking at Smurf as if he had lost his mind. The plan was to kidnap Black's son and use him as bait to get at Black and kill him.

"That wasn't part of the plan, bro," T-Boy said, driving down the main streets to see police speeding past them on the opposite side of the street.

"You said you was sick of waiting. There you go. I just took care of all of your problems," Smurf said, going to sleep.

T-Boy knew Smurf was going through it. Since he lost Shantell, he hadn't been the same, and T-Boy was worried about him.

Romell Tukes

Chapter 24

Yonkers, NY

Smurf's grandmom and older sister had just walked out of a doctor's office near the downtown area surrounded by tall new skyrise buildings.

"It's going to be okay, Grandmom," Tamara said as they waited for traffic to slow down so they could cross the busy street.

"I know, baby. It's God's plan. I won't be able to live forever, love. Only a cat got nine lives," her grandmom said sadly.

Smurf's grandmom's doctor had just informed her she had bone cancer, which would eventually spread throughout her body and most likely kill her in a matter of months.

"It's just shocking."

"I understand. I know my grandbaby going to be upset about this."

"Yeah," Tamara replied, seeing a ticket man writing her a ticket.

"Don't tell Smurf just yet. I want to wait until its good timing, okay, especially after he just lost his girlfriend."

Smurf had moved his sister and mom out of the hood and into a nice mini mansion paid in full and stocked with new furniture, kitchen supplies, food, and wall to wall carpet with a security camera system.

"Excuse me, sir, why am I receiving a ticket? My hour on the meter isn't even up yet," Tamara asked the ticket man.

"This is personal." Black shot Tamara in her face. Her grandmom tried to run off in slow motion to save her own life. She was no fool.

Boc! Boc! Boc! Boc!

Black shot her four times in her back, watching her fall on her face, experiencing a slow death.

Black saw no witnesses as he took off in broad daylight, making his getaway to where Flow was waiting for him around the corner.

***

Brooklyn, NY

Smurf was on Flatbush Avenue with his cousin Biggz, shooting dice with over a hundred niggas outside. Smurf had already lost 10K on so he was done, unlike Biggz, who had a bad gambling habit.

"Yo, Biggz, how that shit moving out here?" Smurf asked Biggz, who was sitting on the hood of his new sky blue lambo with rims and tints, talking to a redbone chick with a phat ass.

"That shit fire, son, word to mother, boy. That shit got fiends rocking up and down the block," Biggz stated.

"Good. That's from Cali, son."

"Damn, bro, I ain't know you had the Cali plug," Biggz said, walking towards him. Biggz had moved back to Flatbush to take over his hood's drug trade and now he had it on lock that's to his cousin putting him on big time.

"I don't. I just know people that know people. But we in Club Love tonight? I gotta head back home after that brotty," Smurf said. He saw two niggas arguing over the dice game, telling each other to suck each other's dick, a sign of disrespect in Brooklyn. One of the niggas left walking off like he was going to get something.

"I'ma get going to meet Chill in East New York before these niggas get crazy," Smurf said.

"I'ma follow you," Biggz said, before answering his phone.

"Hurry up," Smurf added, seeing a nigga pistol whip another nigga.

"Damn, Mom, okay, he right here. We're on our way!" Biggz yelled.

"What happened?" Smurf asked, seeing the crazy look on Biggz's face.

"Tamara and Grandmom in the hospital. They got hit up. Come on, we have to go," Biggz said as Smurf jumped in his BMW, racing down the block with Biggz behind him.

***

Bronx, NY

Days later

Smurf had plans to bury his sister and grandmom both in Harlem, where his grandmom was born and raised around the Malcolm X era. The loss of his grandmother hurt him so much he couldn't leave his crib for three days. His grandmom was a strict church woman who raised him well until he turned to gangs and the streets for a different type of guidance. Smurf always promised his grandmom one day he would give his life to the Lord and that still was on his conscience.

The past two days, Smurf had been paying close attention to Black. He knew it was Black who killed his sister and grandmom in retaliation for his son. Smurf wanted to make Black feel his pain before he killed him, so he was following Kartina around. She looked pregnant with a small pooch on her stomach. It was 10 p.m. and he saw Kartina walking out of an apartment with another woman who was helping Kartina down the stairs and laughing at her.

Smurf watched from across the street in his Honda with a monstrous look in his eyes.

***

Kartina and her best friend Kesha walked to Kesha's truck after spending hours catching up on missed time. Kartina had been so busy with being pregnant and with the death of her son at the daycare that she been over exhausted. Kesha worked two jobs so her life was just as busy. She had no time to chill or go out with friends, so today was special.

"We have to make time to chill again, gurl. I miss your crazy ass," Kesha said, pulling off from her parking spot.

"I know, Kesh. We used to be party animals. Now we old bitches."

"Shit, speak for yourself," Kesha said, laughing.

"Let me find out."

"I'm thirty but feel like eighteen again. I got all types of niggas stalking me," Kesha said.

"Damn, like that?"

"Just the other day I had to call the police about a nigga lurking around my building for two days and you know how much I hate police," Kesha said,

"Facts," Kartina said just as someone rammed into her friend's bumper.

"What the fuck!" Kesha yelled, seeing a Honda behind her with a dent in the bumper from smashing into her. She pulled over next to a gas station.

The man climbed out of the Honda while Kesha opened her door, but before she had the chance to even get out, Smurf was in her doorway.

"Damn, nigga!" Kesha yelled as Smurf lifted his gun, shooting her five times in the breast.

Then he emptied the 9mm Beretta clip into Kartina's pregnant body. She was frozen in shock at what she was seeing.

Chapter 25

Downtown L.A.

The Von Venture Hotel was a nice establishment that charged $1500 a night, but it was worth the stay with a Jacuzzi, spa downstairs, personal chefs, and a view of the City of Angels.

Ryan grinded his python snake deep into Julie's tight soaked pussy as she began to take short breaths.

"Ohhhhh, Ryan," she moaned, spreading her legs wider while she toyed with her tiny clit.

"You like that dick?" Ryan asked as his throbbing dick opened her tight hole.

"Yessssss!" she screamed, biting into a pillow.

Ryan dominated her, pounding her little pretty pussy out the frame.

"I'm cumming, Ryan!" she yelled while his hard pumps grew quicker and more forceful. "Oh shit, I love youuuuu!" she shouted, climaxing with tears in her eyes because the dick was so good.

Ryan then lowered himself to her pussy and licked the slit of her pussy, turning her on.

"Ooohhh yeahhhhh," she moaned, feeling his long tongue fuck her pussy with no mercy. "I'm cumming again, Ryan." Her body began to vibrate and shake as she fucked his finger and tongue while a river of cream leaked out onto Ryan's face and hand.

Julie was exhausted. She lay back on the hotel bed, watching Ryan walk to the bathroom. Ryan came out of the bathroom shirtless, cleaning his handsome face with a warm washcloth showing his chiseled body, which made him look young.

He had met Julie years ago when she first came to L.A. When he saw how beautiful she was, he had to have her, and he did. She eventually met Sousa and he tricked on her millions of dollars, catching her in his web, but what Sousa didn't know was that she was still and would always be in love with Ryan.

"You miss me?" she asked him, blushing.

"Why wouldn't I, love?"

"Just making sure," she said with stars in her eyes.

"What's been going on?"

"Sousa wants you dead, along with whoever the kid is you have with you, Ryan. They say you killed Diego and Dario. Is that true?" she asked when he laid down next to her.

"Yes. They want my son and I won't let them take him alive."

"You have a son?" she asked, unaware, looking at him with an appalled look.

"Yes. It's something I kept a secret and close to my heart to protect him."

"I wonder how many more secrets you have," she said, rolling her sexy eyes.

"Wouldn't you like to know?"

"Yes, I would."

"My secret is you."

"Oh, is that right? Well, my pussy walls say different. You can't keep having me go back with my pussy stretched out. He can tell the difference. His dick is only but so big, baby," she said, trying not to laugh.

"Not my fault I'm blessed."

"Whatever. But I need you to be safe because my husband wants you dead and you know how he is!"

"I do. So, are you willing to set him up for me?" Ryan asked, seeing her hesitate.

"Place and time," she said seriously.

They fucked for a couple of more hours before they both went different ways.

Ryan knew he had to take care of Sousa soon or he would be a bigger problem than he already was. Julie was his personal insider to Sousa's organization. Sousa had no clue Ryan was fucking his wife and then sending her back home to him.

***

New York City, NY

Andy walked out of his lawyer's office in the heart of the city. Andy kept a lawyer on retainer just in case something was to go wrong. He learned that early in the game. He stressed things like that to T-Boy, Force, and Spice because there was no point in hustling if you got locked up with nothing, not even money for lawyers' fees.

Two nights ago, Yonkers PD raided his spot on School Street. He bailed five of his little homies out, but two ratted and were still locked up in Valhalla County Jail.

Andy wore a nice clean black Armani suit with a pair of Cartier glasses and a Cartier princess cut watch worth $78,000. He couldn't help but see the beautiful Spanish woman climb out of the backseat of the white Rolls Royce Phantom with tints double parked in front of his Benz CLA.

"Excuse me, beautiful. It's bad enough you stole my heart but boxing me in will make it hard for me to get away," he said, seeing her blush.

"Maybe I don't want you to get away, papi," she replied, catching him at a loss for words.

Andy loved her strong Spanish accent, but her beauty was different. Her skin was a bronzed tan and she had long jet-black hair, hazel eyes, thin eyebrows, curves, a nice smile, and high perfect cheekbones. Andy had never seen a woman so flawless.

"You okay?"

"Yes, I'm sorry. I'm Andy."

"I'm Maryanna."

"You're honestly breathtaking," Andy said, looking her up and down, checking out her curves in her black strappy dress and six-inch heels.

"Thanks, papi. You're very handsome. I have to go. Let me tell my driver to move" she said, waving at her Spanish driver, telling him to move back so the Benz could get out.

"Thank you. Can I reach you? I would love to see you again. I don't know your situation but I just want to get to know you."

"Take my card, and maybe we can meet up one day," she said, going into her black Birkin bag to pull out a card.

"Okay. Have a good day."

"You too, papi," she said, walking into the lawyer's office.

Andy stared at her ass and was impressed at how phat it was. He had a feeling it was fake but prayed to find out soon.

Chapter 26

Macarthur Park, Cali

"This shit is good," Wolf said, sitting outside of Tommy's Burger spot in the hood near the dangerous Queens Road. The food spot was 24/7 hours and had the best food in town with hotdogs, fries, and chili dogs.

"This the spot, fool. Me and the homies come here almost every night," Largo said, surrounded by eight of his shooters, all enjoying their meals.

"I bet y'all ain't got this shit in Brooklyn," one of the Mexicans said in bad English, wearing baggy jeans and a T-shirt.

"I'm not from Brooklyn. I'm from Yonkers," Wolf stated, correcting him because everybody thought he was from Brooklyn.

A group of Piru Blood members walked up towards the crew, embracing Largo like they were allies. The Bloods looked at Wolf, wondering why he was with a group of MS-18 because he looked Black and Spanish, but they said nothing and ordered their food. They were coming from a house party.

It was 1 a.m. and you could hear loud music in the lot, mainly Nipsey Hussle and J-Roc booming through car speakers.

"All you New Yorkers sound the same to us, fool," Largo said, making everybody laugh.

"I hear you," Wolf said. He saw two cars pull into the lot with tints, making him tense. Ever since losing Big Loc, he had been on extra point.

"You good, fool? Why you look so spooked?" Largo asked.

"You strapped?" Wolf asked.

"Fool, we all strapped," Largo replied, watching Wolf stand up, pulling out his Glock 27 with a 30-round clip, making his way to the two vans.

Boc! Boc! Boc! Boc! Boc! Boc! Boc! Boc!

Wolf shot up the van only to find out it was bulletproof.

Then all hell broke loose. Close to thirty Mexicans with black flags rushed out with military assault rifles. Largo and his crew fired first, but they knew they couldn't hold the powerful assault rifles off for too long. They were in a vicious gun battle when the unthinkable happened. The Bloods saw one of their own get hit by a stray bullet and went crazy. The twenty Bloods joined the MS-18 in the shootout, taking out all the Mexicans in the black flags.

There were so many bodies everywhere you stepped that most likely you was stepping on someone's corpse. Wolf shot two Mexicans he saw hiding on the side of an older pickup truck.

Two cop cars raced into the lot, but when their cars got hailed with bullets, they put their patrol cars in reverse. Unfortunately, one cop got killed.

Largo and his crew hopped in their low riders and the Bloods did the same thing. Wolf pulled off in his Audi, hearing sirens from all types of directions, but Largo led his crew through the back alleys and side blocks.

The Bloods went the other way, bumping into the police, leading to a big police chase all over the city.

***

Yonkers, NY

T-Boy had just come from fucking a thot he recently met on Elm Street, and she was a waste of a fuck. She had a cute face and a phat ass, but the bitch's pussy smelled like a swamp with dead fish in it.

T-Boy had to go meet up with Beans across town on Lawrence Street to speak to him because word in the street was one of their traps spots got raided a few weeks ago, and Beans got out of jail that same night he was arrested. That seemed suspicious to T-Boy, who was going to squeeze the truth out of him some way, somehow. He told Andy he would handle it because he knew he and Smurf had a lot going on with Black and Lingo Loc. Plus T-Boy was the one who put Beans on, so he knew he had to be the one to approach the situation.

T-Boy pulled into the dark park to see Beans's old BMW M2 parked near a trashcan. T-Boy saw him waiting, rocking his feet on the bench like a little kid who had done something wrong and knew he was in trouble.

Beans was about to turn eighteen years old. He was fat, short, with crooked teeth, a lazy eye, and a big bald spot in the middle of his head. He was a hustler. He knew how to get to a bag. His pops was a bigtime dope boy until he got knocked and ratted on thirty-two niggas for his own freedom. Bean's father ended up with sixty years in the feds anyway after snitching.

"Beans, what's good?" T-Boy said, showing no affection.

"T-Boy, what's up? Why you call me down here?" Beans asked nervously, about to stand up.

"Nigga, sit down," T-Boy demanded. "I feed you, nigga. I gave you a place to stay when your crackhead moms kicked you out. I put money in your pockets when your shit was full of lint, son. You snitched. That's the thanks I get?"

"T-Boy, it's not like that. I swear I didn't snitch on you. They only asked about Smurf and Andy," he stated, being honest. The police said nothing about T-Boy because he wasn't their target.

"What did you tell them?"

"They asked about a couple of cop killings, but I told them I didn't know nothing about that. They asked about the chick who got killed on the hill in the car and I told them either Andy or Smurf did it," he said nonchalantly.

"You fucking lame!" T-Boy said, about to reach for his gun until he felt a cold barrel to his head.

"You are too easy," Black said from behind T-Boy.

"Bitch-ass nigga," T-Boy told Beans, who set him up.

"Good looking, Beans. You can go." Black had met Beans the other day. Black knew Beans worked for T-Boy, so he offered to pay him 100K to bring T-Boy to him. Beans knew T-Boy would be trying to kill him, so it was a perfect deal for Beans.

"You got my money?" Beans asked.

Black looked at him like he was crazy before Black blew his brains out. "Where Andy and Smurf?"

"Suck my dick!" T-Boy shouted, pissed off.

"Okay. Have it your way, gangsta."

Boom! Boom!

Black walked off, leaving two big holes in T-Boy's head from his 50 cal hollow tips.

Chapter 27

Hollywood Hills, Cali

Sousa was in his condo, standing over his terrace, drinking a glass of rum, in deep thought. He had thirteen guards inside the large 14.7-million-dollar condo he rarely used.

Trying to kill Ryan and son was harder than he thought. When Sousa found out the kid from New York that was at the top of the hit list was Ryan's son, he couldn't believe how small the world was.

He had recently sent thirty of his men at Wolf and the MS-18 crew, even his nephew, only to have them come back dead. Sousa knew he had to think of something fast or his life could be next.

When he heard the doorbell ring, he walked back into his polished living room, where he had a private bar area.

"Let him in, dummies!" Sousa yelled, hearing the doorbell ring again.

Cruz walked inside the large condo with six big guards, all standing over 6'5" in height.

"Nice place," Cruz said, hugging Sousa, his longtime friend.

"Muchas gracias."

"Pour me a drink while you over there. I'll take a rum and Coke on ice. What's new, Sousa? How's the wife and life treating you?" Cruz asked, taking off his blazer and sitting on the peanut butter leather couch.

"The family is good. I'm just dealing with this Ryan bullshit and his son. It's never been so hard to kill someone. It's like these fuckers got an angel on their shoulders," Sousa said, passing Cruz his drink and sitting down across from him.

"This is the City of Angels."

"So, they say."

"I'm forming a plan now to take care of our little problem, but it may take time. I know the right person to go to," Cruz said.

"Who?"

"Marie?"

"Oh, I don't think so. She's in love with him and if we lay a hand on her, the clap back is going to be too much to handle," Sousa said, worried because Marie was connected to some very powerful people.

"Who says we have to use violence, Sousa? Sometimes it's all about what a person got in there head. I'm a master at mind games so I'm sure she will be easy to feed and act off of impulse."

Sousa nodded his head.

***

Calabasas, Cali

Paola walked downstairs to the indoor pool area in her mom's house. It was a rainy day outside so it was the best time to go for a swim, but Paola had just stopped by to check on her mom.

Sophia was doing laps up and down her pool until she saw her daughter. "Paola, baby, what brings you by?" Sophia said, climbing out of the pool dripping in water with her long brunette hair slicked back. Sophia was beautiful for fifty years old. She was Mexican, brown-skinned, petite, no fat, nice perky breasts, almond-shaped eyes, and a nice bright smile. Most people got Paola and Sophia confused for sisters. Growing up, Paola's mom normally treated her like a sister instead of a daughter.

"You look amazing," Paola said, looking at her mother's nice perfect curves and flat stomach before she wrapped her towel around her body.

"You got a glow, baby. Who's the guy?" Sophia asked, knowing her daughter.

"If you must know, nosy, he's from New York, cute, and we got a good connection. I really like him," she admitted.

"Ohhh, it's about time," Sophia said, smiling.

"Yeah, yeah, whatever."

"How's your brother?" her mom asked, already knowing he was somewhere up to no good.

"South Central."

"That boy needs to grow up," Sophia said, seriously disappointed in her son.

Sophia had her maids cook a big Mexican meal for her and Paola. They enjoyed their meal and their girls' night out.

***

Hollywood Hills, Cali

"I want to warn you, Sousa these photos are over our pay grade, so we want extra. You and Dario hired us to keep eyes on Ryan and take him out, but that went wrong. You never told us how dangerous Ryan was along with his sidekick," said a cop from the Ramp Park police station.

"How much?"

"50 grand," another cop stated.

"They better be worth 50K," Sousa said strongly, reaching for the envelope, but one of the cops snatched it back.

"Money first, amigo," the white cop stated.

Sousa looked at one of his guards and gave him a head nod. When the cops got the stack of money, they handed Sousa the photos they had been taking for the last three months. When Sousa saw the first photo, he thought it was a dream. He saw a photo of Julie coming out of a hotel in L.A. holding hands with Ryan.

"Fucking bitch!"

"Yeah, when we saw her, we knew she looked familiar," a cop said, smiling.

"I can't believe it," Sousa said, going through all the photos of Ryan and Julie coming out of different hotels from all over L.A.

"We'll leave you with that, Sousa. When we take him down, you'll be the first to know."

"I better and bring me his fucking head!" Sousa said, pissed off.

"We will. Make sure you take care of your wife. She may be the missing puzzle piece," one of the cops said, standing up to leave.

"I'ma handle her. You just handle your part," Sousa said.

Chapter 28

San Quentin Prison, Cali

Ryan wore a fresh clean gray new Brook Brothers suit with a pair of designer shades. Ryan walked through the big prison visiting area metal detectors trying to get cleared for his surprise visit to an old friend on death row to find some answers. He spent two hours of waiting, being searched, frisked, piss tested for dirty urines, and his name run in the database for any warrants and felonies. The guards finally led Ryan to a private booth area for death row inmates because they were not allowed to have physical contact. Death row inmates weren't able to hug or touch their mothers, kids, or anyone else who came to visit.

The visits were held in a booth containing a stool to sit on and a telephone to talk to their visitors while looking through a glass window. San Quentin only had thirteen booths to serve more than a hundred inmates. Ryan waited on his visitor and after thirty minutes of waiting, he heard a metal steel door unlock and open. An older man with a short haircut, thick mustache, short, nice build, glasses, Mexican features, and cold eyes came in the booth shackled, waiting for the guards to take the chains off his wrists and ankles.

"Ryan," Ruiz stated before sitting down, rubbing his wrists, watching the guard take the chains out the room. Ruiz picked up the phone.

"Nice to see you, Ruiz."

"I would say the same but I'd be lying, Ryan, and I'm not a liar," Ruiz said, giving him an evil look, letting him know he knew everything that'd been going on.

"How long you got on the Row left?" Ryan asked.

"Whenever the Lord calls for my old soul. I'm 75 years old. I lived my life, Ryan."

"I understand."

"Why, Ryan?"

"Someone wanted to kill my son and hired me to do it, so I'm looking for answers."

"What if the answers aren't the ones you want?"

"What do you mean?" Ryan asked. He knew Ruiz didn't waste his breath on saying things without a valid reason.

"You're going after the wrong people, Ryan. My people didn't pay to have your son murdered," Ruiz said seriously.

Ryan knew Ruiz was an honest man and lived with honor. "So who did?"

"That's a question you have to dig deeper into, Ryan, but does the name Emilio sound familiar to you?"

"Yeah, he used to be a Black Hand out here."

"Yes, but now he lives on the East Coast, hiding out. He will be very hard to find, but he may have the answers you need. Some powerful people reached out to me to have you go kill the Wolf kid. They knew he was your son somehow, so I refused to be a part of that and I told the other families not to get involved," Ruiz stated, looking him in the eyes when he spoke.

"Damn it!" Ryan said, banging his fist on the table.

"You killed my people for nothing, and now you and your son's days are numbered, Ryan. I treated you like my own. You should have come to me first before you went to the point of no return."

"I can't cry over spilled milk."

"Nor can you drink it," Ruiz added.

"I guess this is it."

"I guess so, Ryan. Good luck. No hard feelings."

"One thing you taught me: never take business personal," Ryan said, watching Ruiz lean back in agreement nodding his head.

"It will never be over until you're dead, Ryan. No man is untouchable - not even me."

"True, but the difference between me and you is I'm already dead," Ryan said, getting up to leave.

***

Brooklyn, NY

Black was packing up his bag full of guns and money in a low-key hotel in Redhook he had been staying at for a couple of days. Since Kartina and his unborn seed were killed, he had been emotional, depressed and stressed. He lost everything he had and loved in a matter of months thanks to greed. Black had nothing now except money and drugs on the streets, but that didn't take away the hurt and pain he was suffering from.

Once everything was packed and ready to go with him to Queens, all he could think about was Smurf and Andy. Black opened his hotel door.

"Freeze, FBI!" A gang of agents stormed the hotel in riot gear, tackling Black to the ground like they were at an NFL football game.

Black was cuffed and tossed in a fed van. He wanted to cry. He had never been arrest. He had always beaten the system.

***

An hour later

Black was somewhere in Brooklyn at a federal building in an interrogation room, staring at a middle-aged black man in a suit.

"Mr. Jackson - I'll just call you Black, the famous bank robber. We have been watching you for years but never caught you. You never had a record until you recently caught a traffic ticket and your name appeared in our database. But we know you've been doing much more than violating traffic laws. We have credible information that can tie you to several bank robberies and one of them led to the death of a teller," the agent said, reading his file.

"It wasn't me."

"Yes, it was. We have DNA, photo recognition, and five witnesses. You're facing up to seventy years," the agent said.

"What if I had some info on some big murders across Yonkers?"

"We might be able to get you back on the streets tonight, depending on how good it is. Yonkers has been our number one target lately, but nobody comes forward."

"I know everything," Black said, starting from the beginning.

Chapter 29

Beverly Hills, Cali

Paola and Wolf were in the Westwood Inn, which was the most expensive hotel in Beverly Hills, going for $5,000 for two nights. Paola climbed in the Jacuzzi near the hotel's tall glass windows overlooking over Beverly Hills. Wolf wanted to spend some private time with Paola, so this was perfect the suite was beautiful.

Wolf stared at her sexy body as she moved in closer to him with a glass of Patron in hand, feeling tipsy. Wolf wasn't a drinker, but he had a couple of shots and was horny, feeling the strong liquor.

"Why you always stare at me like that?" she said, blushing, now face to face to with him.

"You're sexy and you win my heart."

"I think I love you," she said, waiting for a reply.

"I think I do too," he replied, moving in to kiss her soft lips. Wolf tongued her down for a few seconds because she was a good kisser. She made everything passionate. That's what turned him on. Within seconds, Wolf was sucking on her neck.

"Ummmm," she moaned, putting her glass down, grabbing his broad shoulder then sliding one hand down to his hard penis. "Fuck me, Romeo," she moaned, knowing tonight was the night she been waiting for and dreaming of.

"I will, baby," he said, undoing her bikini strings, popping out her beautiful titties, sucking on her small brown nipple. He took off his Louis Vuitton swimming trunks.

The warm Jacuzzi water felt so good at the moment. Neither one of them wanted to get out, especially on second base. Wolf placed her body in the corner, lifting her up by her ass, which was wider then he thought and soft. She wrapped her legs around him as the top of his dick entered her sex box.

"Ohhhh," she moaned, holding on to his neck feeling him slow grind his hips deeper into her.

"You too tight. Loosen up. I won't hurt you," Wolf said, feeling her tight pussy walls locking up on him before he could get halfway in her. Wolf took his time until she loosened up and started to fuck her, but then she started going crazy.

"Uhhh, yesss, fuck me!" she screamed. She bounced up and down, making sex faces like a porn star.

Wolf did what she asked. He rammed his dick in and out of her good pussy. "Shitttt," he moaned, unable to go any deeper with his long strokes that had her begging for more and more.

Once they came on each other, Paola wanted back shots, which was her favorite position, so she wasted no time in bending over and grabbing the edge of the Jacuzzi. "Have no mercy, papi, and put your thumb in my, butt, zaddy," she said.

Wolf saw her arch her back and held her ass, shaking his head at how phat it was. He slid his dick in her gushy pussy and rammed himself into her.

"Uhhhh, fuck, ugggghhhh!" she screamed.

Wolf started to fuck her brains out. He slid his thumb in her tiny asshole, making her go crazy. Wolf let her throw her ass back on his, almost making him cum, but he controlled his not and pinned her down. Wolf pounded her back out.

"Ohhhh my fucking God, I'm cumminggg!" she screamed, breathing hard, unable to catch her breath as he came hard.

Wolf pulled out and sat on the edge on the Jacuzzi.

"Where you going, papi? I ain't done," she said, opening his legs, placing his hard dick between her lips and sucking the tip. She made her way deeper down his shaft.

"Ummm," Wolf said, closing his eyes, letting her do her thing. Paola wasn't a pro at sucking dick, but she could make a nigga cum in seconds.

She tried deep throating as much as she could, picking up the speed, giving him sloppy head while doing tongue tricks. When she felt him cum, she continued to suck his dick, catching his cum, which tasted good. She spit it out back on his shaft and deep throated him, holding her head at his base for six seconds, then coming back up.

"Damn, Paola, let's finish this on the balcony," he said, making her jump out of the Jacuzzi to show her freaky side.

***

Bronx, NY

Black and Flow were riding around in Flow's new Ben G-Wagon truck all gray with tints. The two were on the way to Harlem to meet with a plug to talk prices with a Muslim nigga, Ya Ya, who was the biggest kingpin in Harlem.

"Where you been at, bro? Me and Trap was a little worried about you. We know you been going through a stress phase because of what happened, but we here for you, son," Flow said, speeding through the poverty section of the Bronx.

"I'm good, bro, just holding my head. What was the name of son you killed last year in St. Nick?"

"Major and his crew."

"Nah, but you did Major dirty."

"Yeah, I shot him ten times right front of his son. I should have killed his son too," Flow bragged.

"Facts. You did a good job killing them Elm niggas."

"Hell yeah, bro. I ran up in the crib on some man from the fifth floor, shit, killed all them clowns. We been whacking shit over there left and right. Shit, I lost count how many niggas we killed."

"Nigga, we? That's all your work, bro."

"Okay, facts. But you should have seen how I killed a nigga on Weeks Avenue last night. One head shot – boom! Clean hit, bro. Nigga owed Trap money," Flow said.

"Oh yeah? Tell me more, son," Black said, listening to Flow's story, wearing a wire the Feds put on him to keep him out of jail, and he was delivering.

Flow talked about seven murders he committed, unaware everything he was saying would be used against him at trial.

Romell Tukes

Chapter 30

Yonkers, NY

Smurf and Biggz had Lingo's stepsister in the hotel, both performing sexual acts on her, and she was loving it.

"Mmmmmm," she moaned with a mouth full of dick while Biggz fucked her from behind with no type of respect.

"Suck that dick, bitch," Smurf said, guiding her head up and down on his pipe, watching her suck fast and slow.

It was easy to get Namio open for a threesome. All she needed was some molly and Cirôc. This was of one of many threesomes so she was a pro at taking dick in every hole.

Biggz grabbed her waist, trying to control her, but the way she way she was backing her ass up, he almost fell backwards. With every thrust, Biggz made sure he pounded her shit out, making her lose focus on sucking dick.

"Ohhhhh fuck!" she screamed, climaxing at the same time Smurf shot his load down her throat, which made her cum harder.

Biggz continued to fuck her. Smurf went in the bathroom to clean himself because they had been fucking her for three hours straight. They did every sexual move invented on earth. Two minutes later, Smurf came out the bathroom to see his cousin eating her out as she laid on her back, moaning and biting her lips with her eyes closed.

Smurf shook his head because he had nutted in Namio's pussy over five times tonight. He even pissed on the bitch. And now Biggz was sucking cum out her pussy. Smurf got dressed and patiently waited until Biggz was done, but when he saw Biggz kiss her, he knew Biggz was out of pocket.

"Bro, you wilding," Smurf told Biggz.

"What?" Biggz asked, smiling, knowing what he was talking about, but he didn't care.

"We gotta go," Smurf told Biggz.

"Can I come?" Namio asked with excitement, thinking she was a part of the crew.

"Fuck no! You stay put. I got Force and his crew coming through for you," Smurf said.

"How many? I only got one pussy, Smurf."

"That can fit two dicks inside," Smurf added.

"I thought you loved me," she said, making Smurf laugh so hard he fell to the floor

"Bitch, that molly got you tripping," Smurf said, getting up from the floor to leave.

"I'll be back later, baby," Biggz told Namio in a low-pitched voice, about to kiss her.

"Don't you do it, or you walking back to Brooklyn. That's on the gang," Smurf said catching Biggz in his tracks.

"You got that," Biggz said, leaving the room so they could head to Brooklyn to handle some business.

They left Namio there with the sad face, waiting for Force and his crew to come run a train on her again.

***

Bronx, NY

Erica was leaving her doctor's clinic after her daughter's monthly check up and today Erica found out her daughter had bad allergies. The doctor prescribed some medication for her to pick up from a CVS pharmaceutical store. Motherhood was amazing for Erica. It was the life she always dreamed of. Andy played his role as a father and helped out changing diapers and feeding.

She pulled into the CVS parking lot and grabbed her baby, making her way into the store with her daughter in the stroller.

"Excuse me, I'm here to pick up a new prescription for my daughter, Page Harrison," Erica told the older man in the lab coat, who typed the name into the computer.

"Okay, yes, it just got here. Let me get it ready for you. I will need ten minutes. You can have a seat over there," the man said, pointing to the chairs on the wall.

"Thank you," Erica said. "Where is your rest room?" she asked. "Behind aisle eight."

"Okay," Erica said, walking off, pushing Page, who was asleep. Page slept most of the day except when she was hungry. Then she would cry until Erica or Andy feed her.

Erica had to take a piss. She'd been holding it for close to an hour now. She saw how dirty the bathroom was with tampons with blood everywhere, shit stains in the toilet, and dirty tissue everywhere. "Welcome to the Bronx," Erica said, knowing how nasty and dirty Bronx bitches were. She parked the baby stroller near the door before she covered the toilet with new tissue.

While she was pissing, the door flew open and the baby stroller slammed onto the floor. Lingo pointed a pistol at Erica's face with a crazy look in his eyes. Erica was so shocked and numb she couldn't say a word. Page was crying, still in the baby stroller on the floor.

"You wasn't even going to wash your pussy, was you? Nasty bitch!" Lingo shot her in the head and picked up the stroller, rolling it outside, passing civilians looking at the cute, crying baby, proud to see a father in a kid life.

Once outside, Lingo saw a big dumpster and tossed the stroller and Page inside the trash. Lingo hopped in his black Mustang, racing off with no remorse for what he'd just done. The only thing he regretted was not killing the baby. He'd been following Erica for a week now. He could have killed Andy, but he wanted him to feel the saw way he felt when Andy killed Ariana.

Romell Tukes

Chapter 31

Chino Hills, Cali

Largo took Wolf out to a big party at his homie's house, which was big and turned up to the max. Wolf saw everybody doing drugs hardcore drugs like ice, PCP, coke, dope, and crystal. The party wasn't his type of environment, but he stuck around for Largo, who was fucked up.

"Largo, you good, son?" Wolf asked, seeing him on the couch with three bitches, sniffing heroin off the table.

"Huh?" Largo looked up at Wolf, not knowing who he was.

"You know who I am?"

"President Obama," Largo said with a long slur, making a couple of his homies laugh because they all knew how fucked up Largo got, especially on his birthday.

"I think this fool needs to go home. His baby momma just called looking for him and the bitch is crazy, so we out," Largo's cousin told Wolf over the loud Mexican gangsta rap music.

"A'ight," Wolf said, seeing Largo's homies help him up. Outside they were eight deep, walking down the hill to their cars with Largo, letting the air sober him up. Wolf was about to say a joke then out of nowhere, gunmen jumped out shooting.

Wolf covered for Largo and fired back, hitting twos shooter.

Boc! Boc! Boc! Boc! Boc!

Four of Largo's men were dead in the middle of the street. Largo let off a couple of wild shots, missing the gunmen, but hitting one of his homies in the thigh.

Boc! Boc! Boc! Boc! Boc!

Wolf got two more gunmen, but Largo caught a bullet to the neck, dropping him on the side of a red low rider. Wolf shot the shooter who hit Largo seven times. He kneeled down, ducking bullets, trying to help Largo, seeing him hold the hole in his neck, but he was bleeding heavily.

"Go, fool. It's my time," Largo said, taking his last breath.

"Fuck!" Wolf shouted, hopping up, shooting at everything in sight, hitting four targets before he took off with the two MS-18 who were left standing in the gun battle with him.

***

South Central, Cali

Mario was leaving a chick's crib, walking to the Ferrari he had parked in a nearby alley garage that belonged to one of his homies. Mario was from a gang called Avenues who ran a large ring of prostitution and drug trafficking. Mario's mom was rich. He didn't need to live the kind of lifestyle he did, but he was addicted to the streets. His sister Paola told him all the time to leave the streets alone, but he never listened. He was supplying his homies with money to buy drugs and weapons and in return, he was considered down. With two bodies under his belt, he felt like a true killer.

When he turned into the alley, a Cadillac truck was coming his way and stopped in front of him. Five Mexicans hopped out with handguns.

"What's up, fool? You're in the neighborhood," a short Mexican said with a black flag tied around his head.

"I'm good in any hood, buster," Mario said, making the crew laugh.

The short gangsta shot Mario in his leg.

"Ahhhhh!" Mario yelled, jumping on one leg, feeling the pain in his right shin bone. Mario fell on the ground, unable to stand up.

"That shit burn, don't it, fool?" another Mexican said with a laugh.

"Let's kill this fool so we can go get some beers," another Mexican said, aiming his gun at Mario's head.

Boc! Boc! Boc! Boc! Boc! Boc!

All five bodies dropped in seconds and a gunman stepped out of the shadows. Mario though he was seeing shit as the sniper walked his way. Mario tried to crawl away from the shooter, thinking he was next.

"You good, son. I just saved you. I saw you needed help," Wolf said, standing in front of Mario.

"Man, who the fuck are you?" Mario said, bleeding heavily from his leg.

"I'm the nigga that's going to get you to a hospital. We may have to go to a hospital in Glendale," Wolf said, helping Mario up. Luckily, Wolf's Audi was parked around the corner.

Wolf took Mario to the hospital and waited for him. Wolf had been coming from Makartor Park with his dad when he saw Mario cornered in Big Loc's hood where Wolf was still living and fucking with the Crips. At first Wolf was going to mind his business until he saw the dude Paola had showed him as her brother in a couple of pictures she carried around.

An hour later, Mario came out with a cast and crunches. Paola walked into the waiting area wearing pajamas with her hair in a fuzzy ponytail.

"Oh my God, Mario, you okay?" Paola rushed her brother, not even see Wolf sitting down.

"I'm okay, Paola, thanks to him. This dude saved my life," Mario said, looking at Wolf.

"Romeo!" Paola said, confused to see Wolf.

"You know him?" Mario asked.

"Yeah, he's my boyfriend."

"No way," Mario said.

"I have to go. I'll see you tomorrow. Paola. Take care, Mario," Wolf said, kissing Paola's lips and then leaving.

"Paola, he saved my life. He killed five niggas like it was nothing."

"What? Him? Are you sure?"

"Yeah, Paola. Whoever he is, that fool a different type of animal," Mario said, limping on the crutches out the hospital.

Paola couldn't believe what she was hearing. Her mind started to race. Maybe she didn't know the man she loved as well as she thought she did.

Romell Tukes

Chapter 32

Yonkers, NY

"Fuckkk!" the young man moaned, leaning backwards on the sink of the bathroom in the crack house.

Bella was bopping her head up and down on his dick, almost sucking the skin off his cock. She deep throated him like it was nothing and slowly worked her way back up to the tip, doing tongue tricks on the slit of his dick until he couldn't take it anymore.

"Mmmm," she said, smushing his thick, nasty-looking semen all over her face.

Bella had been sucking dick and fucking drug dealers all over Yonkers and Peekskill for a hit. She had turned into a full-blown heroin addict. Her friend Christina was in the living room letting Force and his crew run a train on her.

Force worked for Andy, but he was a big name in Yonkers. He and his right hand Demond both had a large amount of bodies under their belts.

"All done."

"You and your girl need to come around here more. We always here," Dirt said, fixing his clothes while Bella cleaned her face.

"Okay, but can I have my payment?" Bella said with her hand out, not trying her small talk.

"Oh damn, yeah, my bad. You still got a nigga legs shaking. I never seen a fiend so sexy around here," Dirt said honestly, passing her two bundles in a small rubber band with a stamp of a wolf face on all twenty bags.

"A wolf?" she said.

"Yeah. Between me, and you I heard he's like some crazy killer or hitman out here. They say he like a ghost but when he pops up, niggas is dying," he said.

"I heard someone talking about him earlier," Bella said, stuffing the dope in her bra

"Yep. But what's your name anyway?"

"Jenny."

"Like Jenny from the block? I see why. But next time you going let a nigga fuck that phat ass?" Dirt asked, grabbing a handful of her soft ass.

"Maybe. Come right or don't come twice."

"Oh, I'ma cum," he replied leaving the bathroom. He walked into the living room to see four niggas smoking weed with assault rifles everywhere along with keys of coke and dope.

"You ready, Jenny?" Christina said, jumping up, trying to walk straight but unable to because they put a hurting on her. The crew had fucked Christina in the asshole back-to-back. They even let OG Dice, a crackhead, fuck her, but they made sure he went last because word was he had AIDS and was on his death bed.

"Yeah, I'm ready."

"Why you look so familiar, shawty?" Force asked Bella, staring at her from the kitchen.

"Oh, me?" Bella said as Christina's eyes widened.

"Yeah, you."

"I don't know. I used to work at the Cross-Country Mall," Bella said, looking at Force's shirtless chest covered in tattoos. Force was tall, handsome, brown-skinned, tatted up, with waves and a chiseled lean body. The women loved him.

"A'ight, y'all be safe out there." Force looked at her, wondering where he had seen her at because he had never been to the Cross-Country Mall.

Bella and Christina had enough dope for the evening, so they went back to Peekskill.

***

MDC, Brooklyn

Flow had just gotten arrested ten minutes ago while he was driving through Redhook coming from a bitch's crib. When he saw the police lights, he thought it was a regular traffic stop and he was clean, so he pulled over, only to be ambushed by federal agents from every direction. The blocked his Maserati in with trucks and vans as if he was El Chapo's son.

"Mr. Taylor," a black FBI agent in suit said, walking up to Flow to see him lying on the cold steel bench welded to the wall of the jail cell. "You better get used to this type of shit. The feds is ten times worse then up north, trust me."

"Why am I here?"

"Here you go. I'm sure you can read. This will tell you every-thing. The good news is that you're at the top of the indictment. But was it worth it? I mean, the fame and the clout? I don't think so," he said, walking off laughing, leaving Flow to read his charges.

Flow was sick when he saw he had seven counts of murders and eight more counts of conspiracy to commit murders. Flow couldn't believe what he was seeing. He felt like his life had finally been snatched from under of him.

When his cousin Melly from Cortland Avenue got locked up, he called upset and hurt. Now Flow felt all his pain. There were no way he could beat the feds with murders - maybe a 922 (g) (1) gun charge. But this would get him an elbow, or a couple of elbows. Snitching wasn't in his blood. He preferred to do pushups in a cell and make Ramen noodle soup in his cell sink and write letters to his family.

**

L.A.

"Where we going, baby?" Julie asked Sousa as they rode in a bulletproof Tahoe SUV on the dark roads outside of L.A. Julie started to see lots of woods and trees away from the city. Sousa told her they had a special night, so she was eager to find out what he had in store, but she felt a weird vibe from him.

"It's a surprise. I owe it to you," Sousa said, staring out his win-dow with his hand on his chin.

"Okay," she said, looking into the rearview mirror. She saw one of the guards in the front seat whom she was very close to because they were both Hondurans give her a look telling her to run.

The truck was turning up a private road leading into the woods. Julie opened the door and jumped out with the truck still moving. Sousa grabbed her hair, but only got a handful of tracks as she took off.

"Get her!" Sousa yelled to his guards.

Julie was already across the highway with her heels off, dashing through the dark woods barefoot.

The guards stopped before going into the woods because there were all types of mountain lions and coyotes up there. Sousa was pissed that she got away. He had plans to torture her, get Ryan and Wolf's location, and then kill her.

Chapter 33

Yonkers, NY
Weeks later

Biggz waited for Smurf at the Metro North train station in his lambo, impatient. He had no clue where Smurf was coming from, but he wanted Biggz to pick him up from the train station. Biggz was in Yonkers fucking with his side bitch who used to live in Brooklyn. She was a big girl, but she had some wetty.

Since Biggz's grandmom and cousin Tamara were killed, Smurf had been acting odd and tonight, Biggz was going to push the issue. The death shocked the family, but they had to hold shit together and chase a bag.

He was parked under a small bridge. It was dark outside, and Biggz wanted to head back across town. He hated riding around Y.O. with a gun, especially in a lambo. The police harassed niggas in Hondas, so he was a target.

Biggz rolled his driver's side window down and lit a Newport, taking long drags. He heard a train coming above his head. He checked his AP Audemar diamond face watch, seeing it was 9:15 p.m.

"Sir?" a male voice said, creeping up on Biggz.

He thought it was police when he stuck his head out his window.

Boom! Boom! Boom!

Lingo left three in Biggz's dome, leaving his head dangling on his door panel.

Lingo ran off to his Ford Explorer SUV, going the opposite way, seeing civilians get off the train. Lingo knew Biggz's side bitch. He went to school with her. He paid her 100K to tell him where Biggz was at.

***

Smurf walked downstairs with a backpack full of explosives he had bought from his Harlem nigga Jet, who was a gun and explosive dealer. Walking outside the train station, Smurf saw all types of police and a crowd of civilians watching the police put up yellow tape with the corners. Smurf looked for Biggz. His heart was racing at a rapid speed because he knew if he got caught with all the shit he had in his bag, he would be in ADX in Colorado under the jail cell.

"What happened?" Smurf asked a white chick, looking over the crowd, being nosy.

"It looks like a fat man - African American, of course - got killed in a new lambo. The car is nice. I wonder how much drugs he sold to get that. Hey, do you have any weed for sale?" the white chick, who looked like a hippie, asked.

Smurf walked off feeling his heart sink because it was his fault. He got Biggz killed. But he didn't want to drive or take a cab with a bookbag full of TNT bombs.

He felt like he was losing control over his life. Everything and everybody he loved or dealt was dying. He walked up the block with his hoodie on, passing niggas on the block hustling, having fun, and living life.

***

Mount Vernon, NY

Andy was on his way to Newburgh to holla at Spice about the next re-up from Trigger because shit was getting low. He was down to five keys. Andy was pushing a BMW coupe with tints. He just watched cars to make sure he wasn't tripping about the Honda Accord following him.

He saw an alley a block ahead and came up with a plan. His phone was going off. When he saw it was Smurf, he knew it would have to wait.

***

"I got this goofy-ass nigga now, boy," Black said out loud to himself. Rain started to come down hard, but that only made Black more eager to shed blood for the deaths of his family members.

He saw Andy make a right into a dark alley. Black knew he had him trap now. Before he passed the alley, Andy jumped into the middle of the road with a Draco, firing shots.

Black didn't see this coming. He flooded the gas pedal, ducking under the wheel, trying to hit Andy and beat the thunder of bullets.

"Ahhhhhh, fuck! Bitch-ass nigga!" Black yelled, feeling a sharp pain in the back of his shoulder.

***

Andy saw the Honda race down the block. He got in his BMW, making his way to the highway, thinking about Black's face. He promised Wolf he wouldn't kill Black, but the rules might have just changed.

***

Queens, NY

Trap answered the jail call to hear his brother's voice on the other end of the line.

"Yo, Flow, I been looking all over for you."

"Trap, get low now."

"What? Why? What happened, son?" Trap asked.

"I got fifteen bodies, and Black is the only nigga I told about a couple of murders. I lied about most of them and son is all in my paperwork my lawyer just gave me."

"Damn, yoooo, I knew something was fishy about boy. I got you, son. I know what's up," Trap said, laughing.

"What's so funny?" Flow asked, tight.

"You remember when I was locked up how you did me? And you don't think I ain't know you was fucking my bitch?" Trap said.

"Nigga. It's not the time for that," Flow said.

"Nah, my G, it is. Blood supposed to be thicker than these hoes. Don't drop the soap, nigga, and you better get you one of them Kufis."

"Suck my dick, nigga!" Flow yelled before hanging up in Trap's ear.

Trap had Flow's girl in his Benz sucking him off.

Chapter 34

Westwood, Cali

Sousa was relaxing in his Westwood mini mansion only few knew about. He came here to party and get peace of mind when needed. His backyard had a pool overlooking the mountains, a small courtyard, a gazebo, and a basketball and tennis court.

Since Julie escaped death, he had his men on a 24/7 hunt for her, but they came up empty every time. He knew she had no family, so there weren't too many places she could go. He had frozen her bank accounts so she had no money to get out of town unless Ryan helped her. He was crushed when he saw the pictures of his wife and Ryan. He wondered how long it had been going on because there were times they would all go out to dinner or events and Ryan would come to his get togethers.

Sousa was sitting in his gazebo area when his five guards dressed like the men in black rushed to him.

"Boss, the security cameras shut down," said his main bodyguard said. He had been working for Sousa for over a decade. He was a trained martial arts specialist.

"What? How is that fucking possible?" Sousa yelled.

"I don't know. Maybe a hacker."

"I don't give a fuck if it was the Virgin Mary! Fix it now," Sousa shouted.

"Yes sir. I'm on it," the main guard said. He turned around to meet a bullet to the head.

The other guards reacted, seeing three shooters ambush them with MPs assault rifles.

Tat-tat-tat-tat-tat-tat-tat-tat-tat!

Boc! Boc! Boc! Boc! Boc!

The guards shot back, but it was useless because Ryan and Wolf gave out head shots like free drinks at the bar.

151

Sousa's mouth was stuck open with fear running through his blood and veins like never before. Julie walked down the walkway in a sexy red dress with heels.

"Sousa, Sousa, Sousa," Julie said, approaching him. "Don't look so dumbfounded."

"You bitch," he mumbled,

"I've been called worse. You see, Sousa, your day was soon coming after you killed my father," she said, seeing the shocked expression on his face. "Oh, you think I didn't know? You're the reason why I came to L.A. - for revenge - and you fell right into my hands. It's amazing how beauty can get you anything you want in life," she said, taking the assault rifle from Ryan. "Wolf, his stash is on the second level in a bathroom behind the mirror. You will see a safe. The code is 6-17-61-8," she said before looking back at Sousa.

"I didn't order the hit on your father. Ruiz did. I was only doing what I was told to become a loyal member of the Five Families."

"Well, look where that got you."

"Spare my life, baby, please. You will never see me again," he begged.

"Oh please! You sound like a pussy," Julie said before shooting Sousa thirty-six times. Tears came down her face because she been waiting on this day since her father's and mother's deaths.

Julie saw Sousa murder her family in cold blood. Her father knew they were coming, so he told her to hide in the living room closet. She watched her family get murdered in the living room and since that day, she never forgot Sousa's face.

"You okay?" Ryan asked, seeing the pain on her face.

"Sí," she said, wiping her tears.

"Come on, let's get out of here. Our work is done," Ryan said, walking off.

Julie had gone to Ryan's house after her escape. She told him how Sousa was about to kill her and formed her own plan with his help. Ryan had no clue Julie knew where he lived because nobody did. That made him wonder, so he asked her. She told him she tailed him many nights to see how many bitches he had and he only had a handful, which he told her about.

Wolf hacked into Sousa's security cameras with ease to shut down the systems so they could get in the house without being detected. Wolf left Sousa's home with close to 250 keys, which he planned to send to Andy tonight.

***

L.A.
Weeks later

Paola and Wolf had just tied the knot. They got married at a small chapel. Wolf proposed to her two nights ago. He was truly in love with her. She was special to him. She felt the same way about him, so she was glad to say yes.

Wolf forgot all about Bella. She wasn't a factor in his thoughts at all. Paola filled her shoes ten times more.

Mario was the best man and Paola's mom was her bridesmaid. Ryan couldn't make it because he was in the Bay Area on business.

Wolf had plans to take Paola to Paris for their honeymoon.

Romell Tukes

Chapter 35

Hollywood, Cali

Cruz's personal driver was at a gas station pumping gas into the new Bentley SUV for Cruz's trip to Las Vegas in an hour. The man walked into the store to pay for the gas, waiting in the long line. After paying the store clerk, the man got inside the SUV, pulling off on his way to Cruz's mansion in Hollywood Hills surrounded by the rich and famous.

"Keep driving," a voice said from behind the driver in the seat. The driver felt a gun to the back of his head.

"I have a family, please! You can have the truck. Just let me go," the driver cried, looking in the rearview mirror at Wolf.

Wolf had sneaked into the truck when the man went inside the store to pay for the gas. Ryan was a couple of cars behind trailing them. Thanks to Julie, he knew where Cruz was hiding out at and he should have known.

"Take me to Cruz, and no funny shit, or your family on 138 Orcha Road, apartment 3F in Glendale, dies," Wolf said, seeing the fear overtake the driver's face knowing his family life was now at risk.

"Okay," the driver said, swallowing a lump of saliva.

"How many guards there?"

"Four outside at the gate and four inside," the driver said, driving through the rich Hollywood Hills.

"Where is Cruz?" Wolf asked, placing a silencer on his 50 cal handgun with a thirty shot clip.

"Him and his wife will mostly likely be upstairs on the third floor preparing for their trip."

"Okay," Wolf said, seeing his dad's Benz a short distance away while he listened in on their earpieces.

"Here we go," the driver said, pulling up to the gates, rolling down his window to see the high gates slowly open.

Wolf shot the driver in the head. Four guards were approaching the Bentley, wondering why Gordo, the driver, wasn't pulling in the driveway. All four men had AK-47 assault rifles in their hands as they got closer.

PSST, PSST, PSST, PSST, PSST, PSST, PSST!

Wolf jumped out, hitting all the guards, clearing the way. Ryan was seconds behind him as they ran through the long narrow driveway to the house with three Bentleys parked near the waterfall. Ryan opened the front door, duck walking inside quietly, to see two guards coming out of the back kitchen area.

PSST, PSST, PSST, PSST, PSST!

Both guards fell face first into the hard marble floor with bullets to the head.

Ryan and Wolf hid on the side of the wall, seeing two guards walk downstairs playing with their earpieces like they had lost communication.

PSST, PSST, PSST, PSST, PSST, PSST!

Wolf took the lead and popped out on both men, hitting them both in their chests, watching their bodies stumble down a flight of stairs.

"Nice shot," Ryan whispered, hearing voices coming from the double doors on the third floor. Ryan kicked the door open to see Cruz and a beautiful Latina woman in lingerie with the body of a goddess. Ryan shot Cruz's wife in her upper torso. Her body collapsed on the large California king-sized bed full of the clothes they were packing for their trip.

Cruz tried to keep a straight face, but his lip and chin were trembling as he stared at Ryan and Wolf.

"Surprise," Ryan said.

"You killed my wife."

"Cruz, who is the man who wants my son and me dead?" Ryan asked.

"You already received your answers from Ruiz. I can't help Ryan, so kill me if you going to kill me," Cruz stated.

"Who is Emilio?" Wolf asked.

"He's in New York. He sent word to us about you, that's all I know. But no matter what you do or who you kill, you're still marked," Cruz said seriously.

"Yeah, that's my life story," Wolf said before hitting Cruz in the face seven times, sending his body crashing into the bedroom wall.

"Looks like all the answers are in New York, kid. Maybe someone sent us on a detour," Ryan said, trying to figure shit out.

"Maybe we going to find out," Wolf said, leaving the gruesome crime scene.

***

Auburn Maximum-Security Prison, NY

CB was in his cell doing pushups and listening to his small boom box, playing an old L.O.X. album, which had his whole tier singing the songs word for word.

"What number you on, young blood?" OG Chuck asked, banging on the wall.

"2600!" CB yelled, out of breath. "What number you on?" CB replied.

"750. I'm an old man. I can't do things I used to except jerk my chicken... pause," OG said, laughing.

"Too much information!" CB yelled back, doing 50 clips pushups to 80 sets.

The prison was on a month lockdown because a young inmate got killed on the yard by a Muslim who had been down twenty years. The young kid only had five years and two left before he went home, but he disrespected the quiet, humble Muslim on the yard for bumping into him. The Muslim waited until the yard cleared and stabbed the kid up over forty times, killing him.

"You got that *Gangsta Qu'ran* paperback by that kid Romell Tukes under Lockdown Publications?" OG asked.

"Yeah, I'ma pass it to you," CB said.

"A'ight. Son can write. He from Yonkers too"

"Facts. I don't even read too many hood books unless it's from Romell or Ca$h and a couple more authors from Lockdown Publications."

"I feel the same. I'm about to make a seafood rice bowl. You down?" OG asked

"Nah, no carbs. Gotta cut this shit up," CB said, passing him the book.

Chapter 36

Bronx, NY

Trap kept a good distance on the silver Lexus LC 500 coupe three cars in front of his black Dodge SRT Challenger Hellcat Redeye muscle car, which was his speed demon. The skies were dark today - not a star in sight, giving the city a darker look. Trap swerved around potholes, trying to keep up with the Lexus coupe, passing Mott Haven projects.

After speaking to Flow weeks ago, it finally hit him that Black could give him up too - if he hadn't already. Trap didn't feel sympathetic for Flow's arrest. Trap had to protect his own life.

He had been following Black for thirty minutes straight when he finally saw the Lexus pull into the back of Patterson projects. Trap parked a couple of cars down from the Lexus. He saw the lot was clear of people and made his move. He pulled his gun out, creeping out of the Lexus to see the driver's side window was down.

Boc! Boc! Boc! Boc! Boc!

Trap fired four shots into the chest of a man who he thought was Black, but he wasn't.

"Try again, muthafucka," a voice said, appearing from the shadows with a gun aimed at Trap's head.

"Fuck!" Trap cursed himself angrily.

"You thought I was lacking, son? Never that, boy. I'm always two steps ahead of my opponents. That's the first rule to the game." Black stood behind Trap, breathing on his neck.

"Your breath smell like shit, nigga," Trap replied.

"I knew you would try to follow me, so I sold the Lexus," Black said.

"Nigga, you a killer rat. At least I'ma die with honor," Trap said hearing Black laugh

"I wouldn't call it ratting. I call it playing for keeps. Only the strong survive and it looks like you're the weakest link.

Boom! Boom! Boom!

The .357 gun blew Trap's head off. Black was gone before his body every hit the pavement.

***

Yonkers, NY

Smurf and Andy were in a low-key condo they were using to stash drugs and guns at because keeping shit in the hood was over. They took too many loses.

"That's 250," Smurf said, looking at all the bricks stacked up on the living room wall, taking up half the wall.

"Facts, bro. Force and Spice on their way to get there hundred. What you want to do with 50?" Andy was dressed in fatigues and Timbs boats, all black.

Bury it or put it in the ceiling for a rainy day, son," Smurf said, rolling up a blunt of sour and kush mixed in one.

"A'ight, but yoooo, we gotta focus on Lingo and Black. We losing too much," Andy said, sitting down.

"Wolf on his way back, right?" Smurf hadn't killed Black, but he was leaving him no choice. Andy promised him he wouldn't kill his brother, not him, so it was all fair game in his books.

"He said he gotta finish some shit up, then he'll be back up," Andy said fed up with Black and the whole situation.

"Does Black even know he really robbing his own brother?"

"I don't know or care, but son got one more time to jump out there and I'ma roll his black ass," Andy said.

***

Highland Park, Cali

Wolf had recently gotten back from his honeymoon in Paris. It was beautiful. They stayed at a beautiful hotel. They went shopping at all the most expensive designer stores and they went sightseeing.

He was on his way to Compton to meet someone named Bloody Red for his father to pick up some money along with info on Emilio.

Things were starting to come to light and Wolf felt like he was getting closer to finding out who was responsible for wanting him dead. He was driving his father's Wraith because Ryan was in Vegas with some chick his father said was a very important woman and he cared for her. Ryan explained to him that if he didn't live such a dangerous lifestyle as a hitman, he would have married her.

Wolf was thriving and he was in the mood for either Wing Stop or Roscoe's, the two best food spots in L.A. Wolf was starting to like Cali, but he was homesick. He hadn't seen a pair of Timbs out here yet. He was so sick of Chuck Taylors.

Last night, Paola begged him to move into her mansion with her in her condo in West Hollywood. Wolf tried to explain he wasn't ready to do that because he didn't want any harm to come to her because of him. His reasoning led to a small argument.

Paola had heard the story Mario told her about the night Wolf saved his life and killed five people over twenty times before she came up with the guts to ask Wolf what type of shit he was really into. While in Paris, she asked him and he told her he lived a dangerous lifestyle and did kill people, and she left it at that.

Wolf stopped at a four way to see that Paola was calling, but when he was trying put the phone on the car speaker, multiple bullets shattered the Wraith's windows. Not waiting to get shot without putting on a move, Wolf hopped out, dumping back at the six Mexicans shooting next to the Ford F-150 pickup truck. Wolf caught two shots to his chest, falling back in his Wraith after he shot and killed two Mexicans on a busy street in broad daylight.

The pickup truck left after completing their mission, hitting Wolf. They had thought it was Ryan in the Wraith, but his son was much better to kill.

Wolf took three deep breaths, ripping off his Teflon vest. Wolf got in the front seat, driving off in pain, hearing sirens blocks away. He was glad he wore the vest Ryan gave him today, but his chest felt like he got shot because the bullets knocked the wind out of him.

Romell Tukes

Chapter 37

Yonkers, NY

Lingo drove through the mean streets of Yonkers, on his way to the Bronx to see a nigga he had been locked up with up north in Wendy prison near Rochester, NY. It was noon out and cold. Lingo hated the winter times in New York because it felt like the North Pole. He was going to cop some guns because he was starting to run out of weapons.

He never imagined coming home to lose everything he loved in a matter of months. Every night he thought about Ariana and all the good times they spent together, but now with only memories left to hold onto, he felt lifeless.

Passing the precinct, he heard a motorcycle roaring behind him, about to pass him, which was rare in the wintertime.

Tat-tat-tat-tat-tat-tat-tat-tat!

The Mack 11 ripped through the door frame, making Lingo lose control of the car and crash into a mailbox and light pole on the corner.

The bike took off on a wheelie, racing off. Smurf pushed the bike to 85 mph until he got back to Elm Street.

***

Ossining, NY

Black was standing over his sister's grave in deep thought, wishing he would have spent more time with Victoria and been a supportive brother. Things hadn't always been sweet with his mom and him, but he regretted letting their relationship affect his brother/sister relationship. He felt like he failed his sister. He always knew she was going to be someone special one day because of her high spirits and energy. When he got the call from Wolf, he cried for two days straight because she didn't deserve to die so young.

Black knew firsthand that bullets didn't have names, but he knew plenty more people who deserved to die instead of her.

The worst part of all this was Black was holding on to a big secret that played on his conscience and dealing with his little brother. Months before Black formed a crew and started to rob Andy's and Smurf's traps, he was watching Wolf. When he started to see his brother making power moves, he knew his greed wouldn't allow him to see past it. Black started to form plans to rob Wolf's spots. He knew Andy and Smurf were his go-to guys, so he placed his attention on them. Black know it was wrong to snake his brother, but he had to eat, and Andy and Smurf weren't his kin or anywhere close.

Black had to slide out to Harlem for the night to check on his trap spot on Lenox Avenue. With Flow and Trap both gone, he knew he had to find a new area and crew. He got in his Porsche 911, leaving the gravesite.

***

Peekskill, NY

Bella was throwing up in the toilet area, feeling dope sick. She hadn't had any heroin since yesterday so she going through with-drawals and her body was aching. Christina was out trying find some drugs for them, but things were dry in Peekskill because the Feds arrested 37 drug dealers.

After vomiting for almost an hour, Bella couldn't take it any-more. She wanted help. She was sucking and fucking for her next hit every day. It was starting to drain her mentally and physically.

Bella made up her mind then and there that she couldn't live like this anymore. She packed up her shit and left, heading to the nearest rehab center.

***

Yonkers, NY

Namio parked behind her apartment building. She was coming from a party in Long Island, which was litty, held at a mansion in the North Hamptons. She had been living her best life, scamming and boosting with her girls. That's how she was able to pay her bills and take care of herself.

Namio wore a Chanel skirt and blouse with red bottom heels, showing her ashy feet and the chipped nail polish on her toes. She walked through the back door of her building, feeling the liquor she been drinking all night. It was hard driving back home from L.I., but she made it safely without getting pulled over or crashing.

"NaNa," a voice said, stopping her in her tracks because only her family called her NaNa.

Lingo stepped out from the laundry room with a pistol in hand and a neck brace and cuts all over his face.

"Lingo," she said, sobering up quickly. Namio feared this day would happen. She had tried to cover up her tracks, but she saw now she didn't do a good job at it.

"You look so surprised, sister" Lingo said with fire in his eyes. He and Namio never had a perfect relationship but she was still family and Lingo never crossed family or friends.

"I'm sorry," she cried out as tears formed in her eyes. Namio was a pro at making herself cry and Lingo knew this firsthand so he couldn't help but laugh.

When Namio saw he was laughing, she knew he wasn't buying it, so she ran towards the back door.

Boc! Boc! Boc! Boc! Boc!

All five bullets landed in her back, making her fall in slow motion with her hands in the air.

"You dumb bitch! You think I ain't know it was you giving the ops my location? You the reason how I got the drop on them niggas," Lingo said, kicking her in her stomach, watching her crawling and bleeding all over the place.

Lingo shot her in the back of the head four times before walking off in pain. The car accident fucked up Lingo's back and he had broken his neck, but he had been waiting to get Namio for the long-est.

Chapter 38

MDC, Brooklyn

Flow was on a lawyer visit, going over two new charges the feds hit him with yesterday. "How can they do this shit?" Flow shouted, going through his new indictment.

"It's two murders, and they have you on video on one of them red-handed. The other one, you left your DNA at the scene," Mr. Gates stated, pulling out stacks of documents from his leather briefcase for his client.

"It wasn't me," Flow said.

"That line's been over since they found your fingerprints at five of the crime scenes, but that's not the main concern," Mr. Gates said, taking off his glasses, which left a red circle on his white pale face.

"What's the main concern? Because it looks like they trying railroad a young black brother."

"You railroaded yourself by killing all these people, and your worry should be the star witness, who is overly eager and willing to testify against you at court," Mr. Gates said seriously.

"Man, it sounds like you more against me than with me."

"I'm with you, but I'm with justice and what's right. I'll help you the best way I can, but to be honest, there is only so much I can do in your situation. The best thing I can recommend is for you to take a plea deal," Mr. Gates suggested.

"A plea deal? And what's that?"

"As you know, you're on a death row hold, but if you willing to cop to life, you will be able to get a direct appeal and file a 2255 motion."

"Let me think about it," Flow said, getting up to leave.

Flow had heard about his brother's death and was hurt. Even though Trap turned his back on him, he was still his brother. There was no doubt in his mind Black was responsible for Trap's death. Flow always knew Black had some type of hidden agenda the first time they met, but Flow was blinded by the fact that he was about to get rich.

On his way back to his unit on the 7th floor, all the time he was facing hit him hard - so hard he wanted to cry out loud. Flow got back to his unit and went to his cell to take a nap to sleep the pain away.

**

Calabasas, Cali

Paola sat up in her bed, listening to Wolf sleep. She looked at the gun in her hand, which belonged to Wolf. Paola found out Wolf wasn't the person who she thought he was. Instead, he was an impostor. She pointed the Glock 40 at his head as it weighed her hand down, ready to squeeze the trigger.

Wolf opened his eyes to see Paola pointing a gun at him. He saw something in her eyes he never saw before. Paola looked him in his eyes and put the gun down.

"Are you cheating on me?" she asked with tears.

"What? No, baby. You was about to shoot me?" he asked, taking her silence as a yes. He took his gun out of her hand and got out of bed. "Baby, I told you I live a dangerous life."

"I know, I was just tripping. I'm sorry," she said, hugging him from behind.

"You can't be doing shit like that, ma. You have to learn to communicate with me when feel any type of way. What if the gun would have went off?" he asked her seriously.

"I know, I wasn't thinking. I'm sorry," she said, looking into his eyes.

They made love for two hours and forgot all about what happened.

**

Las Vegas, NV

"Ahhhhh yessss, Ryannnn!" the beautiful Puerto Rican woman moaned, grabbing the bed sheets while she arched her back in the air, taking back shots.

Ryan held her firm waist, fucking her from behind, making her ass jiggle with every thrust. Her pussy was tight, wet, and phat. The way she worked her pussy walls made it hard for him to control himself in her ocean.

"Yesss, papi!" she screamed. "I'm cumminggg, papi, oh fuckkk!" she yelled, hitting her climax and a high note at the same time. She turned around and started sucking him off so good his body had chills and he started to Harlem shake while cumming in her mouth.

"Damn, baby, I gotta go back in the a.m. You can't hold me hostage in a hotel room. You know what I have going on," Ryan told her.

"I know, papi, but it's like I never get to see you no more," she said, flashing her dark blue eyes at him.

Ryan had been fucking Salma for ten years now, but he had known her since she was twenty years and now she was thirty-five years of age.

Salma was a work of art: 100% Puerto Rican, light skin, thick thighs with a phat ass, long blonde hair, big breasts and 5'6" in height. She was in love with Ryan. She knew he lived a dangerous lifestyle but she could relate. Since she lived on the East Coast, it was hard to come visit daily, so she came out to see him when it was possible.

"Let finish making this night special," she said, grabbing his dick, placing it back in between her large lips and going to work.

Romell Tukes

Chapter 39

Downtown Yonkers, NY

Smurf walked into the large church in his biker suit as Sunday service went on. Lately Smurf had been having dreams of getting saved and changing his life. For some reason he woke up knowing today was that day. He was tired of living a life of violence after he lost everything he cared about in nearly a year's timing. He listened in the back of the church on the wall while an older black preacher jumped up and down shouting, getting the large crowd hyped.

"Can I get an amen?" the preacher yelled.

"Amen!" the crowd shouted.

"I said can I get an amen!"

"Amen!"

"We're here today to testify that there is only one Him. Mmmmmm, we come to testify that He is our savior. Mmmmmm, can I get an amen?" the preacher shouted, jumping up and down.

"Amen!" the crowd yelled, going crazy.

"Who wants to give their life to the Lord today, right now? Come forward. Don't be scared. The power of the Lord knows what's good for the soul. Come get saved," he whispered into the mic as if he was talking to a certain individual.

Smurf felt like that was his calling. He walked forward in slow motion. Each step felt like a step closer to the Lord. He felt like he was walking the Green Mile looking as churchgoers stared at him. Some people clapped, cried, stood up, nodding their heads in approval for the young black man who was about to give up the life of sin.

"Come up here, young man," the preacher said, smiling, wondering why Smurf looked so familiar. But the reason was because Smurf killed his son in the Getty Square shopping area years ago in front of him. The preacher got a quick glimpse of Smurf that day before he took off running.

Smurf stood in front of the preacher.

"You're ready to give your life to the Lord, young man. I see a lot of hurt and pain in your eyes. The Lord will wash it all away!" the preacher screamed, pulling out a bottle of Holy water.

"I'm ready," Smurf stated, feeling like it was the right thing to do with his life.

"Okay!" the preacher shouted, placing both hands on Smurf's small peanut head. He started to scream and shout verses from the Holy Bible for a full two minutes.

***

Everybody from the church embraced Smurf, even the sexy young church girls who thought he was cute and wanted to fuck.

When Smurf left the church, he texted Andy. "Bro, I changed my life and got saved. You should too, bro. I left that life alone. I love you, but I got my calling. I hope you understand." Smurf took a deep breath, hopping on his motorcycle, ready to start a new life. He had money, so he planned to skip town and go to Delaware to start a new life. Smurf hadn't had a good night's sleep since he started killing people and hurting innocent people.

The bike sped out of the church lot on to the main street. A pickup truck came out of nowhere and slammed into the moving bike, tossing Smurf off. The bike slid ten feet, stopping next to Smurf who slowly tried to get up and move, but he had broken his ribs, hip bone, shoulder blade, and leg.

The driver of the truck went to turn Smurf over on his back, checking on him. When Smurf saw Black's face, a wave of fear overcame him.

"Bye-bye."

Boom! Boom! Boom!

Black ran back to the stolen pickup truck, seeing civilians pull up to the other intersection looking at the dead body in the middle of the road.

***

Hollywood, Cali

Wolf was walking out of Lowes with some tools to help Paola repaint he house.

The married life was okay to Wolf because he wanted to grow old with Paola, but lately he could tell something was bothering her. Ever since the night he woke up with his own gun to his face, he was forced to sleep with one eye open. He was waiting on his next move because he was starting to run out of plans. The only thing he knew was a name in New York. He felt like he was starting from scratch again.

He had bought a new Audi A8 yesterday because his dad's Wraith was recently torn into pieces and there was no way Wolf was buying him a new %=$500,000 car.

Wolf hit the push to start button on the Audi to start and saw a sexy tall Spanish woman with brownish skin. She had long curly black hair, hazel eyes, a nose ring, slim toned figure, and pierced dimples. She was pushing a baby carriage. When they made eye contact, Wolf know if he wasn't married he would have bagged her. She wore leggings and Air Max 95, which were foreign in Cali, so he knew so had swag.

He was about to enter his car, but he looked back to get a little glimpse at her ass. When Wolf saw her reach over into the carriage, his dick got hard. But when he saw the Tech 9 sub machine gun, he ducked.

"Crazy bitch!" he shouted, shooting back. His Ruger jammed on him. "Fuck!" he yelled as bullets hit the Audi. The woman was closing in on him, but a gunman came out from the side of a Denali SUV with an SK assault rifle, firing towards the woman, who took off.

The shooter hit the woman in her leg. She was now limping across the parking lot, trying get away. When Wolf got a closer look at the gunman who saved him, he laughed.

"Police will be here. You may want to get off the floor. That crazy bitch almost got you," Ryan said.

"Who was she?" Wolf asked, leaving his shot up Audi and following Ryan inside his SUV.

"Cruz's daughter Audrey. She was in the Navy until now. I forgot to tell you about her. But how about lunch?" Ryan asked as Wolf just looked at him.

Chapter 40

Makartor Park, Cali

Ryan was in his condo elevator, trying to make sense of everything that was going on. Ryan knew he would have to go all the way to New York for answers. He really didn't want to, but he felt he had no choice. Throughout this whole journey he was glad to have met his son and formed a bond. He only wished he could have been there more for him growing up because he knew how it felt to grow up without a father present.

Making his way into his apartment, he felt a funny vibe. He closed the condo door to walk into a trap. He saw over twenty goons with assault rifles aimed at him with red laser beams.

"Ryan, nice to finally meet you," a female voice said from the terrace. When Ryan saw the beautiful young woman he smiled, admiring her body and facial features.

"You look just like your mom," Ryan said, walking past her goons to sit down on his living room couch.

"So, I assume you know who I am and what I'm here for."

"Take a look inside the kitchen counter drawer, the one to your far left," Ryan said, watching her walk into the kitchen.

Seconds later, she came out with a folder, looking through the photos and documents. "So, you knew I would come?"

"Eventually, yes."

"Why not prepare?"

"I'm well prepared, Paola. It's just my time."

"Does Wolf know?"

"Not yet, but he's a smart kid. I'm sure it won't take long for him to figure things out," Ryan stated.

"He'll be dead by then."

"So, you married him…for what?"

"I do love him, but I have to keep my promise," she said, unable to make eye contact because she felt like he was reading his soul.

"Daddy's little girl going make him proud. But imagine what will happen to you if you don't do what Daddy says?"

"When that time comes, I will deal with it."

"You knew when me and your mom was having an affair. Your father found out, and that's when everything went downhill. Ruiz has always been a sucker for love and I got a feeling it runs through his blood. You may kill me, but you don't know what runs through my veins."

"I will find out."

Boc! Boc! Boc! Boc! Boc!

Bullets danced in his chest, making Ryan's body jump with every shot. Paola watched him take his last couple of breaths, smiling, then left with her goons.

Paola was Ruiz's daughter and Cruz's niece. When she went to see her father last month, he explained everything to her from A to Z. He told her she was the only person who could destroy Ryan and Wolf. Paola had no clue Wolf was living this type of lifestyle. When her father told her about all the powerful people he killed, she started to fear for her own life.

The night she pointed a gun to his head she was going to kill him, but she couldn't bring herself to do it.

***

San Quentin Prison

Ruiz was in his cell on the death row tier doing burpees, listening to grown men cry and scream. Most of the inmates had been waiting on their execution dates for close to thirty years.

Ruiz heard his cell phone ring and stopped working out to answer it. He had four correctional guards on his payroll so he lived like a king on death row. The only thing he didn't get was pussy. He answered the new iPhone to see it was his baby girl Paola.

"Good, baby, thank you. Now finish off the rest and be careful, because I got a feeling Wolf is a little more challenging than his father," Ruiz said before hanging up.

Ruiz hated putting his daughter in this type of situation, but since she was a baby he knew she would be a monster. She had the smarts, wits, and beauty to run his organization.

***

South Central, Cali

"Wow, Paola, are you sure going against your husband is a good idea? I told you I saw that nigga kill like he was on a special op mission." Mario was talking to Paola near a beach full of people.

"Mario, we have no choice. Daddy said it needs to be done," Paola said, fixing her bikini line straight, enjoying the Cali heat.

"I don't think we should do it. I'ma ride wit' you regardless, but I think this is a suicide mission. I love Daddy too, but we never going to see him again, and if the Five Families are all killed, that shit's over." Mario shook his head, hoping his sister would see the big picture.

"We must carry our family legacy, and I'm willing to do whatever it takes to take what's ours. I just killed Wolf's father. How long do you think it will take for him to put the pieces all together?"

"You right."

"I know," she said, putting on her Balmain sunglasses, looking into the ocean waves as people surfed and rode jet skis.

Romell Tukes

Chapter 41

LAX Airport
Days later

Wolf had just boarded the airlift on his way back to New York. He couldn't bear to stay in California one more day and he refused to bury his father.

When he had gone to check on his father last week in his condo because he wasn't answering his phone, he got the surprise of his life. He saw Ryan dead on his living room couch with his eyes open. Wolf just left him there because there was nothing he could do except grieve.

Later that night, Wolf found a letter in his car glove compartment. It was from Ryan. When he read it, he was confused, hurt, and angry. Ryan told him by the time he got the letter he would most likely be dead. Ryan told him Paola was Ruiz's daughter and he knew this when he saw them together, but he knew he was in love and Paola had no clue who he really was at that moment, so their love was true and real. Ryan told him Paola would kill him and would eventually come for him, but first he had to finish the mission they started, and all the answers were back in New York.

Wolf had a feeling Paola was up to something since the night he woke up with a gun to his face. The story about him cheating was just a cover-up because he caught her about to blow his head off.

He felt like he helped his father get murked by marrying Paola. He was blinded by her love and beauty. He felt like everything was made up now from the first time he laid eyes on her.

***

Westchester, NY

Salma sat in her living room area, looking at old photos of Ryan and her. She tried to hold her emotions back, but it was too hard. She had puffy eyes and a red nose from crying all night she looked like shit. Her guards were posted up in every corner of her 17,419 square foot mansion.

Salma yearned for revenge. She was going to find out who did this and her reach was so long that it wouldn't take long. Salma was one of the biggest kingpins on the East Coast. She supplied a lot of heavy hitter throughout the Tri-State area. She was Aguilera's sister and Bella's aunt and even though she hated her shady brother, when he was murdered, she was heartbroken.

Her full name was Salma Aguilera. She had her own empire in Puerto Rico, thanks to her ex-husband. She was only married to him for nine months before he was brutally murdered. Salma's ex-husband used to beat on her, rape her, and force her to perform sexual acts on other powerful man. She wanted out so badly, but he had so much power she would never leave alive.

One day she met with Ryan and he helped her form a plan that would forever change her life. Ryan killed her husband and his guards for her. She took over his empire and turned it into her own. Every man her late husband made her perform sexual acts on, she killed and took over their territories and turfs.

She planned to get in touch with Wolf soon to see if he knew anything, but the only problem was she only know his name. She didn't know what he looked like but had her men on a manhunt for him in Cali.

***

Yonkers, NY

Lingo was up early this morning on a manhunt, as usual. Last night he finally got a location on Andy in Albany and he was about to slide up there.

He walked into the corner store and ordered a bacon, egg, and cheese bagel, his regular.

"Yo Ock, make sure the yolk is cooked!" Lingo shouted because yesterday the egg yolk was uncooked.

"Okay," the Muslim man replied, a little shaky, preparing his order on the clean grill.

Lingo had a four-hour ride to Albany so he went and grabbed two Red Bull drinks to keep him up.

Five minutes later, the Ock was at the register ringing up his items. Lingo paid and walked outside, looking up and down the block. He had been very cautious and on point.

Once inside the Porsche truck, he crashed his sandwich and he downed a Red Bull energy drink. Seconds later, Lingo felt dizzy and lightheaded. He passed out in his driver's seat.

***

Andy walked out of the store and put the "We're Closed" sign up after killing the Ock in the store.

When Lingo came in the store, Andy was hidden behind the counter pointing a Glock 17 at the store clerk. Andy placed some strong, powerful sleeping tranquilizers into Lingo's food, knowing he wouldn't make it halfway down the block. Andy had been watching Lingo for two days and knew it would be easy to catch him like this instead of just killing him in public and making a scene.

He climbed in the Porsche, pushing Lingo's body over into the passenger seat before pulling off. He saw high school kids look into the corner store window, wondering if Ock was in the back making salat (prayer).

***

Twenty-five minutes later

Andy saw Lingo's eyes slowly open and he started to panic. Lingo ankles, wrist, and body were tied to the passenger seat so he couldn't move.

"You killed Smurf?" Andy asked.

"No, I swear, bro, please!" Lingo cried.

"You look scared," Andy said, pouring gasoline all over his face and body. Andy had already poured two and a half gallons on the outside of the Porsche.

"Please, man, don't do this. Y'all niggas killed my brother. What the fuck you expect?" Lingo yelled before Andy poured gasoline in his mouth, choking him.

Andy pulled out his Glock with a 30-shot clip and filled his body up with bullets until his gun was empty. Andy was at an abandoned warehouse in the back near a chemical factory, so nobody could hear a sound. He lit a match and tossed it on Lingo's lap, watching his body go up in flames. Andy stood there for a few seconds until the fire started getting wild.

Andy climbed in the G-Wagon Benz SUV he had parked there overnight, pulling off to meet Wolf at the JFK airport. He tried his best not to think about the loss of Smurf. Now he knew that Lingo didn't do it, there was only one person left.

Chapter 42

Auburn Maximum-Security Prison, NY

CB sat in front of four parole board members, chained and cuffed, sitting in a chair. Today was the day he had been waiting on: his hearing for his parole to see if they were willing to give him a chance at freedom. Normally it was rare to get parole on a murder charge.

"Mr. Jackson, we have reviewed your case, which is murder in the first degree, docket number 15rh7281. You are currently serving a 15 to life sentence," a white woman in her mid-forties stated. She had nice green eyes and red hair.

"Yes, I am," CB said, feeling his palms starting to sweat.

"Why should we let you back into society, Mr. Jackson?" a black man with a goatee asked. He wore a nice gray designer suit.

"Sir, I came to prison as a kid. When I did my crime, I didn't have the full attention of what I was doing because my brain was immature. I do take full responsibility for my actions. I've grown and used my mistake as my foundation to become a better person. I feel as if I do deserve a second chance in society. I believe people can change. I'm a firm believer and a witness. Not only have I found God, but I also found myself and my calling, which is to help the youth and other kids who are misled and confused," CB said perfectly. He and OG Chuck had been going over this speech for two weeks now and CB was surprised at how good his acting was.

"Mr. Jackson, I think you deserve an award for that performance, hands down, but I've looked over some prison incidence reports and I see you're a Blood member with high ranking. I also see you're responsible for over twenty cuttings and stabbings in the last year," an old black woman said, giving him the evil eye.

"I don't remember the last time I caught a ticket. I'm being accused for something I never did or know nothing about," CB said, looking in all of their eyes, showing them, he was sincere.

"You can step out and give us a second to make our decision," the white woman stated, looking through his folder.

CB went outside to see a long line outside.

"Yo, son, how they acting? Please don't get them people mad. They going to bang all of us," a fat nigga from Harlem said. He was doing a 50 to life bid for drug trafficking.

"Nah, you good, son. I ain't on that type of time," CB said, hearing his name called inside the room.

CB sat down as the white woman cleared her throat.

"Mr. Jackson, we came to a 3 to 1 vote and we believe…" She paused, seeing the sweat on CB forehead "…that you are, in fact, ready for another chance in society. We do believe in second chances, but in murder cases it's normally a long time before we let out inmates - I mean convicts. We all believe you won't make us regret out choice," she stated.

"Mmmmm," the black woman mumbled, rolling her eyes. She was the only one who voted against CB because she saw his kind every day.

"Thank you so much," CB said, wanting to cry.

***

Yonkers, NY

"Wolf, shit been going crazy out here, bro, but him killing Smurf put the icing on the cake. This right here shows you what type of nigga he is, bro," Andy said, passing Wolf some papers.

"What's this?"

"I got a man in MDC, Brooklyn on a Fed charge and he's on the same block as a nigga named Flow. He was with Black until Black ratted on him. That's all the paperwork, son. Facts. Black no good, Wolf. If he snitched on his own mans, I know we next," Andy said, watching Wolf read the black and white.

Wolf was at a loss for words. He hated snitches. He knew he had to do something quick before he ended up in a jail cell next to Flow.

***

Peekskill, NY

Bella was in her residential rehab center, getting her life back in order. She hated herself for going so low. She would have never imagined she would be doing drugs and worse, turning tricks for drugs. She sat in the group meeting listening to a woman from Newburgh, NY tell her life story, which brought tears to Bella eyes.

"I had nobody to blame but me. Who could I blame for my addiction? Could I blame my father and uncles for raping me every night as a kid? Could I blame the system for taking my mother? Could I blame the police for killing my two sons? Could I blame my ex-husband for killing himself? Could I blame a virus I gave to myself? I can't. Now every day I have to live with AIDs and an addiction. If I can help anybody in this room, I want to tell them to leave that shit alone. It's worse than a bullet hitting your heart because it is a slow death."

After group was over, Bella went to her room to take a nap but when she got inside, she saw a small brown envelope on her bed along with a small tape recorder. Bella opened up the folder to see photos of Wolf with her father at a dinner, at a waterfront, and a bunch of other places. She was overwhelmed because she never knew he was meeting with Aguilera.

She saw pics of Wolf coming out of her father's home the same day he was murdered, which was too hard for her heart to hold. She tried her best not to think negative, but the clues never lied. Deep down she still loved Wolf, but she couldn't let him see her like this. She was truly ashamed of herself.

She picked up the tape recording and listened to it. At first it wasn't clear, but then she started to hear her voice and Wolf's voice. Her father was telling Wolf his days were numbered and some powerful people were after him. Her father told him about some families in Cali who wanted him dead and paid him a lot of money to kill Wolf.

After a couple more seconds of talking, Bella heard the gunshots and tears welled in her eyes. She now knew who was behind her father's death.

Chapter 43

George Washington Bridge, NY

Black was on his way out of town, but the New York traffic on the most occupied bridge in the city with three levels had hours of traffic.

He felt like it was time to get away. He had a feeling the Feds were watching him, especially after Smurf's death. He saw Dodge SUV trucks tailing him. Black was bumper to bumper in a red and black Mustang with dark tints. He had two duffle bags in the trunk, one full of money and the other with all types of guns. Traffic was barely moving. He just put the car in park and played some music, a Fabolus album.

He saw a Jamaican nigga with long dreads and a crown walking on the bridge with sunglasses. Black paid him no mind because he knew how crazy New Yorkers were, especially Jamaicans and foreigners. Black didn't even see his car door fly open until the Jamaican nigga jumped in his passenger seat with a gun pointed at him. Black was so caught in the moment he didn't even realize who was behind the sunglasses.

"You dumbass nigga," Wolf said, slamming the chrome 45 pistol across his brother's face.

"Wolf, come on, man."

"You knew those were my spots?"

"Wolf, that was a mistake, man, you gotta believe me," Black begged, bleeding from his head.

"To make shit worse, you're a vicious rat"

"What? Who told you that?"

"Too late to cop the fifth, bro."

Boom! Boom! Boom! Boom!

Wolf hopped out of the car, racing away on foot just as traffic started to move. He got in his stolen cab and pulled into traffic, forgetting about the dead Jamaican he had killed and tossed in the backseat like he was taking a nap.

***

Staten Island, NY

Weeks later

Wolf looked at the rundown apartment, wondering what type of Mexican leader - or ex-Mexican leader - would even spend a night in this dump in the middle of the hood.

Months ago, he had received this address from Ryan before his wife killed Ryan. He thought about Paola every night. He felt betrayed, lied to, used, and violated. Out of all people to kill, he found it crazy how his wife could kill his father cold-bloodedly with no remorse. Deep down he knew he was next, but Wolf was more than ready now. He thought about the night she had the gun to his face and all he could think about was what stopped her from killing him.

Wolf got out of the used Toyota and made his way into the building, which had a strong odor in the lobby, like a nursing home hallway.

Emilio's apartment was on the first floor at the end of the long hall. Wolf saw the apartment door was wide open with music playing in the backyard. It was Mazes Frankie Beverly "Can't Get Over You".

Wolf walked into the polished, clean apartment that was hooked up with new floor rugs, furniture, and fresh flowers everywhere. Nobody would ever imagine a crib this fancy in this rundown building, and that's why Emilio loved it.

Wolf saw a short Mexican man dancing in his living room with a glass of tequila in his hand. Emilio directed Wolf to take a seat while he was still two-stepping like he was in the club. Wolf had never seen an old Mexican nigga with so much swag. He wanted to laugh so badly while sitting down, but he kept his game face on because he needed answers.

Emilio eventually turned the music down and looked Wolf up and down. "So, you Wolf, huh?" Emilio asked, pouring himself another drink.

"Must have known I was coming?"

"You damn right. I know everything," Emilio said, finally sitting down, taking a deep breath. "Put your gun on the table," Emilio asked and Wolf did so with no complains.

"I got some questions."

"I know you do, but before we start, I want to play a little game as we go along with your questions and I will give you all facts." Emilio pulled out a .357 handgun, taking out the bullets and placing one in the chamber.

Wolf looked at him like he was crazy. He had no type of intentions to play with his life. This was literally suicide.

"No worries. I play alone. People always ruin the fun," Emilio said, smiling.

"First question."

"You only have five, so make them good," Emilio stated strongly, taking a sip of his tequila.

"Why do people want me dead?" Wolf asked. Emilio put the gun to his own head and pulled the trigger to get a click.

"Man, you wilding," Wolf said in shock because he thought he was faking.

"You're a piece to someone's missing puzzle. Someone has been pulling your strings since your sister's death, and now they see they can't use you no more. You're dead weight, just like how they did me."

"I don't understand?" Wolf said, not realizing he had just asked a second question.

Emilio placed the gun to his head again and pulled the trigger to feel the click.

"Aguilera had no clue the person who paid him to kill you knew all along you would sooner or later kill him. Aguilera and your person of interest used to fuck around until greed got in the way."

"So, who is this fucking mystery person that's been trying get me killed and paying Mexican leaders to get me whacked?" Wolf asked the biggest question of his young life.

Emilio picked up the gun and pulled the trigger against his head to get another click, leaving Wolf's heart racing.

"Now this is the game changer, kid, because the person behind all of this is very powerful, rich, deadly, and sneaky. You would have never figured it out unless you came here. I was the one giving the money and word to send to the Five Families in Cali, but the person that wanted you and Ryan to kill each other must have got soft. Back in the day he would killed his own father for money - which he did. Anyway, your own mother Rita is the one who set up everything. She is a powerful woman. She tried to have Ryan killed, but he killed her assassins and spared her life. Rita supplies the East Coast and down south with dope and coke. She did a good job at hiding it from you, Vic, and Black, but CB found out years ago, Wolf. Your mom won't stop until you're dead," Emilio said, seeing Wolf's amazed facial expression.

"Why would she kill my little sister? It don't make sense?" Wolf saw Emilio pick up the gun, putting it to his head.

Boom!

Emilio's blood splattered all over the walls and his body slumped onto the couch.

Wolf got his gun and tried to stand up, but his feet felt numb. He couldn't believe what he just heard. When he could move again, he left the apartment, trying to add everything up, because never in a million years would he think his mom was behind this. He hopped in his car, pulling off on a new mission.

To Be Continued...
Killers on Elm Street 3
Coming Soon

Submission Guideline

Submit the first three chapters of your completed manuscript to ldpsubmissions@gmail.com, subject line: Your book's title. The manuscript must be in a .doc file and sent as an attachment. Document should be in Times New Roman, double spaced and in size 12 font. Also, provide your synopsis and full contact information. If sending multiple submissions, they must each be in a separate email.

Have a story but no way to send it electronically? You can still submit to LDP/Ca$h Presents. Send in the first three chapters, written or typed, of your completed manuscript to:

LDP: Submissions Dept
Po Box 944
Stockbridge, Ga 30281

DO NOT send original manuscript. Must be a duplicate.

Provide your synopsis and a cover letter containing your full contact information.

Thanks for considering LDP and Ca$h Presents.

Romell Tukes

BOW DOWN TO MY GANGSTA

By **Ca$h**

TORN BETWEEN TWO

By **Coffee**

THE STREETS STAINED MY SOUL **II**

By **Marcellus Allen**

BLOOD OF A BOSS **VI**

SHADOWS OF THE GAME II

TRAP BASTARD II

By **Askari**

LOYAL TO THE GAME **IV**

By **T.J. & Jelissa**

IF LOVING YOU IS WRONG... **III**

By **Jelissa**

TRUE SAVAGE **VIII**

MIDNIGHT CARTEL IV

DOPE BOY MAGIC IV

CITY OF KINGZ III

By **Chris Green**

BLAST FOR ME **III**

A SAVAGE DOPEBOY III

CUTTHROAT MAFIA III

DUFFLE BAG CARTEL VI

HEARTLESS GOON VI

By **Ghost**

A HUSTLER'S DECEIT III

KILL ZONE **II**

BAE BELONGS TO ME III

A DOPE BOY'S QUEEN III

By **Aryanna**

COKE KINGS V

KING OF THE TRAP III

By **T.J. Edwards**

GORILLAZ IN THE BAY V

3X KRAZY III

De'Kari

THE STREETS ARE CALLING II

Duquie Wilson

KINGPIN KILLAZ IV

STREET KINGS III

PAID IN BLOOD III

CARTEL KILLAZ IV

DOPE GODS III

Hood Rich

SINS OF A HUSTLA II

ASAD

KINGZ OF THE GAME VI

Playa Ray

SLAUGHTER GANG IV

RUTHLESS HEART IV

By Willie Slaughter

FUK SHYT II

By Blakk Diamond

TRAP QUEEN

By Troublesome

YAYO V

GHOST MOB II

Stilloan Robinson

KINGPIN DREAMS III
By Paper Boi Rari
CREAM III
By Yolanda Moore
SON OF A DOPE FIEND III
HEAVEN GOT A GHETTO II
By Renta
FOREVER GANGSTA II
GLOCKS ON SATIN SHEETS III
By Adrian Dulan
LOYALTY AIN'T PROMISED III
By Keith Williams
THE PRICE YOU PAY FOR LOVE III
By Destiny Skai
I'M NOTHING WITHOUT HIS LOVE II
SINS OF A THUG II
By Monet Dragun
LIFE OF A SAVAGE IV
MURDA SEASON IV
GANGLAND CARTEL IV
CHI'RAQ GANGSTAS IV
KILLERS ON ELM STREET III
JACK BOYZ N DA BRONX II
A DOPEBOY'S DREAM II
By **Romell Tukes**
QUIET MONEY IV
EXTENDED CLIP III
THUG LIFE IV
By **Trai'Quan**

THE STREETS MADE ME III

By **Larry D. Wright**

IF YOU CROSS ME ONCE II

ANGEL III

By **Anthony Fields**

FRIEND OR FOE III

By **Mimi**

SAVAGE STORMS III

By **Meesha**

BLOOD ON THE MONEY III

By J-Blunt

THE STREETS WILL NEVER CLOSE II

By K'ajji

NIGHTMARES OF A HUSTLA III

By King Dream

IN THE ARM OF HIS BOSS

By Jamila

MONEY, MURDER & MEMORIES III

Malik D. Rice

CONCRETE KILLAZ II

By Kingpen

HARD AND RUTHLESS II

By Von Wiley Hall

LEVELS TO THIS SHYT II

By Ah'Million

MOB TIES II

By SayNoMore

BODYMORE MURDERLAND II

By Delmont Player

THE LAST OF THE OGS II

Romell Tukes

Tranay Adams
FOR THE LOVE OF A BOSS II
By C. D. Blue

Available Now

RESTRAINING ORDER **I & II**
By **CA$H & Coffee**
LOVE KNOWS NO BOUNDARIES **I II & III**
By **Coffee**
RAISED AS A GOON I, II, III & IV
BRED BY THE SLUMS I, II, III
BLAST FOR ME I & II
ROTTEN TO THE CORE I II III
A BRONX TALE I, II, III
DUFFLE BAG CARTEL I II III IV V
HEARTLESS GOON I II III IV V
A SAVAGE DOPEBOY I II
DRUG LORDS I II III
CUTTHROAT MAFIA I II
By **Ghost**
LAY IT DOWN **I & II**
LAST OF A DYING BREED I II
BLOOD STAINS OF A SHOTTA I & II III
By **Jamaica**
LOYAL TO THE GAME I II III
LIFE OF SIN I, II III
By **TJ & Jelissa**

BLOODY COMMAS I & II

SKI MASK CARTEL I II & III

KING OF NEW YORK I II,III IV V

RISE TO POWER I II III

COKE KINGS I II III IV

BORN HEARTLESS I II III IV

KING OF THE TRAP I II

By **T.J. Edwards**

IF LOVING HIM IS WRONG…I & II

LOVE ME EVEN WHEN IT HURTS I II III

By **Jelissa**

WHEN THE STREETS CLAP BACK I & II III

THE HEART OF A SAVAGE I II III

By **Jibril Williams**

A DISTINGUISHED THUG STOLE MY HEART I II & III

LOVE SHOULDN'T HURT I II III IV

RENEGADE BOYS I II III IV

PAID IN KARMA I II III

SAVAGE STORMS I II

By **Meesha**

A GANGSTER'S CODE I &, II III

A GANGSTER'S SYN I II III

THE SAVAGE LIFE I II III

CHAINED TO THE STREETS I II III

BLOOD ON THE MONEY I II

By **J-Blunt**

PUSH IT TO THE LIMIT

By **Bre' Hayes**

BLOOD OF A BOSS **I, II, III, IV, V**

SHADOWS OF THE GAME

TRAP BASTARD

By **Askari**

THE STREETS BLEED MURDER **I, II & III**

THE HEART OF A GANGSTA I II& III

By **Jerry Jackson**

CUM FOR ME I II III IV V VI

An **LDP Erotica Collaboration**

BRIDE OF A HUSTLA **I II & II**

THE FETTI GIRLS **I, II& III**

CORRUPTED BY A GANGSTA I, II III, IV

BLINDED BY HIS LOVE

THE PRICE YOU PAY FOR LOVE I II

DOPE GIRL MAGIC I II III

By **Destiny Skai**

WHEN A GOOD GIRL GOES BAD

By **Adrienne**

THE COST OF LOYALTY I II III

By Kweli

A GANGSTER'S REVENGE **I II III & IV**

THE BOSS MAN'S DAUGHTERS I II III IV V

A SAVAGE LOVE **I & II**

BAE BELONGS TO ME I II

A HUSTLER'S DECEIT I, II, III

WHAT BAD BITCHES DO I, II, III

SOUL OF A MONSTER I II III

KILL ZONE

A DOPE BOY'S QUEEN I II

By **Aryanna**

A KINGPIN'S AMBITON

A KINGPIN'S AMBITION **II**

I MURDER FOR THE DOUGH

By **Ambitious**

TRUE SAVAGE I II III IV V VI VII

DOPE BOY MAGIC I, II, III

MIDNIGHT CARTEL I II III

CITY OF KINGZ I II

By **Chris Green**

A DOPEBOY'S PRAYER

By **Eddie "Wolf" Lee**

THE KING CARTEL **I, II & III**

By **Frank Gresham**

THESE NIGGAS AIN'T LOYAL **I, II & III**

By **Nikki Tee**

GANGSTA SHYT **I II &III**

By **CATO**

THE ULTIMATE BETRAYAL

By **Phoenix**

BOSS'N UP **I , II & III**

By **Royal Nicole**

I LOVE YOU TO DEATH

By Destiny J

I RIDE FOR MY HITTA

I STILL RIDE FOR MY HITTA

By **Misty Holt**

LOVE & CHASIN' PAPER

By **Qay Crockett**

TO DIE IN VAIN

SINS OF A HUSTLA

By **ASAD**

BROOKLYN HUSTLAZ

Romell Tukes

By **Boogsy Morina**
BROOKLYN ON LOCK I & II
By **Sonovia**
GANGSTA CITY
By **Teddy Duke**
A DRUG KING AND HIS DIAMOND I & II III
A DOPEMAN'S RICHES
HER MAN, MINE'S TOO I, II
CASH MONEY HO'S
THE WIFEY I USED TO BE I II
By Nicole Goosby
TRAPHOUSE KING **I II & III**
KINGPIN KILLAZ I II III
STREET KINGS I II
PAID IN BLOOD **I II**
CARTEL KILLAZ I II III
DOPE GODS I II
By **Hood Rich**
LIPSTICK KILLAH **I, II, III**
CRIME OF PASSION I II & III
FRIEND OR FOE I II
By **Mimi**
STEADY MOBBN' **I, II, III**
THE STREETS STAINED MY SOUL
By **Marcellus Allen**
WHO SHOT YA **I, II, III**
SON OF A DOPE FIEND I II
HEAVEN GOT A GHETTO
Renta
GORILLAZ IN THE BAY **I II III IV**

Killers on Elm Street 2

TEARS OF A GANGSTA I II

3X KRAZY I II

DE'KARI

TRIGGADALE I II III

Elijah R. Freeman

GOD BLESS THE TRAPPERS I, II, III

THESE SCANDALOUS STREETS I, II, III

FEAR MY GANGSTA I, II, III IV, V

THESE STREETS DON'T LOVE NOBODY I, II

BURY ME A G I, II, III, IV, V

A GANGSTA'S EMPIRE I, II, III, IV

THE DOPEMAN'S BODYGAURD I II

THE REALEST KILLAZ I II III

THE LAST OF THE OGS

Tranay Adams

THE STREETS ARE CALLING

Duquie Wilson

MARRIED TO A BOSS... I II III

By Destiny Skai & Chris Green

KINGZ OF THE GAME I II III IV V

Playa Ray

SLAUGHTER GANG I II III

RUTHLESS HEART I II III

By Willie Slaughter

FUK SHYT

By Blakk Diamond

DON'T F#CK WITH MY HEART I II

By Linnea

ADDICTED TO THE DRAMA I II III

IN THE ARM OF HIS BOSS II

Romell Tukes

By Jamila
YAYO I II III IV
A SHOOTER'S AMBITION I II
By S. Allen
TRAP GOD I II III
By Troublesome
FOREVER GANGSTA
GLOCKS ON SATIN SHEETS I II
By Adrian Dulan
TOE TAGZ I II III
LEVELS TO THIS SHYT
By Ah'Million
KINGPIN DREAMS I II
By Paper Boi Rari
CONFESSIONS OF A GANGSTA I II III
By Nicholas Lock
I'M NOTHING WITHOUT HIS LOVE
SINS OF A THUG
By Monet Dragun
CAUGHT UP IN THE LIFE I II III
By Robert Baptiste
NEW TO THE GAME I II III
MONEY, MURDER & MEMORIES I II
By **Malik D. Rice**
LIFE OF A SAVAGE I II III
A GANGSTA'S QUR'AN I II III
MURDA SEASON I II III
GANGLAND CARTEL I II III
CHI'RAQ GANGSTAS I II III

KILLERS ON ELM STREET I II

JACK BOYZ N DA BRONX

A DOPEBOY'S DREAM

By **Romell Tukes**

LOYALTY AIN'T PROMISED I II

By Keith Williams

QUIET MONEY I II III

THUG LIFE I II III

EXTENDED CLIP I II

By **Trai'Quan**

THE STREETS MADE ME I II

By **Larry D. Wright**

THE ULTIMATE SACRIFICE I, II, III, IV, V, VI

KHADIFI

IF YOU CROSS ME ONCE

ANGEL I II

By **Anthony Fields**

THE LIFE OF A HOOD STAR

By Ca$h & Rashia Wilson

THE STREETS WILL NEVER CLOSE

By K'ajji

CREAM I II

By Yolanda Moore

NIGHTMARES OF A HUSTLA I II

By King Dream

CONCRETE KILLAZ

By Kingpen

HARD AND RUTHLESS

By Von Wiley Hall

GHOST MOB II

Stilloan Robinson
MOB TIES
By SayNoMore
BODYMORE MURDERLAND
By Delmont Player
FOR THE LOVE OF A BOSS
By C. D. Blue

BOOKS BY LDP'S CEO, CA$H

TRUST IN NO MAN

TRUST IN NO MAN 2

TRUST IN NO MAN 3

BONDED BY BLOOD

SHORTY GOT A THUG

THUGS CRY

THUGS CRY 2

THUGS CRY 3

TRUST NO BITCH

TRUST NO BITCH 2

TRUST NO BITCH 3

TIL MY CASKET DROPS

RESTRAINING ORDER

RESTRAINING ORDER 2

IN LOVE WITH A CONVICT

LIFE OF A HOOD STAR

Romell Tukes